MEET SAM SPACE...

the best private eye on this or any other Earth. Trained in seventeen forms of solar combat, he can snap the trunk of a small pine tree with a double reverse dropkick...providing his shoes are on. He broke a toe once trying it barefoot. He's also a sucker for a pretty girl's sob story...even if she does have three heads. After all, numbers don't count—it's what you do with the body beneath. And when the solar system is threatened with final destruction, the body beneath teams up with Sam on an impossible journey to the planets and across time in one of the wildest and funniest science fiction novels ever written.

D0828700

SPACE
FOR HIRE

BY WILLIAM F. NOLAN

A CRIME CLASSIC

INTERNATIONAL POLYGONICS, LTD.
NEW YORK CITY

To Sam's great-grandfather,
for sentimentally hardboiled reasons.

Library of Congress Card Catalog No. 84-80781
ISBN: 0-930330-19-6

Printed and manufactured in the United States of America
First IPL printing April 1985
10 9 8 7 6 5 4 3 2 1

INTRODUCTION

This book was first published thirteen years ago—and was honored by the Mystery Writers of America with a Poe Special Award scroll as one of the five best original paperback novels of 1971. However, its publisher, Lancer Books, went out of business shortly after printing SPACE FOR HIRE, and the book never got the audience it deserved. I was flattered by the fact that it became a sought-after collector's item, but I was disappointed by its short lifespan on the newsstands.

Now, at last, SPACE FOR HIRE is back in print from IPL, along with a brand new sequel novel, LOOKOUT FOR SPACE. Once again, my hard-knuckled private eye from Mars is happily punching and shooting his way around the galaxy.

Sam is a direct reflection of my enthusiasm for old pulps, early Warner Bros. gangster films, and, of course, the wondrous landscape of science fiction. He's Bogart in a space helmet, blasting his way out of the *Black Mask* era into the World of Tomorrow, popping in and out of alternate universes, bedding down robots, being captured by mice, laying eggs, and generally raising merry hell on a dozen planets. He's hypnotized, seduced, slugged, double-crossed, tortured, brainwashed, drowned and fatally shot. Among other things.

Sam's adventures form a unique cross-mix of mystery and science fiction, and I trust that readers in both fields will find him as much fun to read about as I did to write about.

Personally, I love the big lug.

My thanks to Hugh Abramson of IPL for bringing him back to life.

William F. Nolan
Agoura, Calif.
1984

One

I was bored.

It was one of those long hot lazy Martian afternoons when you don't give a damn about anything. I had some paperwork to do on a Saturn time machine swindle but I was in no rush to get at it.

I was perched behind my desk, feet up, my head tipped back, speculating on the progress of a Martian sandworm who was intent on crossing the ceiling of my office. I was timing him, having made a bet with myself that, at his present rate of speed, it would take him exactly six Earthminutes to reach the far wall.

That's when she came in.

Now, as an Earthman, my taste in females is basic: I prefer just two legs, two breasts and one kisser—but I'm not prejudiced, because a ripe Venusian triplehead can do a lot for me. And this one was ripe.

She stood in front of my desk and leveled three cool pairs of liquid-green orbs at me—along with a neat little nearnickelplate .25 Webbley-Stanton double-thrust paralysis beamer.

I promptly forgot the sandworm and raised both hands.

"Are you Samuel Space?" she asked in a dulcet triplethroated tone.

I nodded. "If you're here to pull a heist all I've got in the office is a bottle of imported Scotch. One-third empty."

7

"Prove it," she said.

"Prove my Scotch bottle is one-third empty?"

She shook her three heads. "No. Prove that you're really Sam Space."

I lowered my hands slowly. Then I stood up, produced my wallet and tossed it on the desk in front of her. "It's all there. License. ID cards. The works."

"Please keep your hands palm-down on the desk," she told me. The beamer didn't waver; it was leveled on my tummy. I did as she asked, since I hate having a paralyzed stomach.

She poked her free hand among my papers. "They could be faked." Four of her eyes looked up at me; the other two continued to scan my credentials.

"But they aren't," I said.

"I happen to know your personal history, Mr. Space. Tell me about yourself. I'll decide if you're lying."

I shrugged. "Okay, sister, I'll give you the two-bit rundown. I'm an Earth op working Mars, a sun-scarred, hard-souled ex-rocket jockey out of Old Chicago, U.S.A. I've boozed the asteroids and brawled my way from Pluto to the rings of Saturn. My parents wanted me to study interstellar law but I always had a yen for travel. So I beat my way through the System. For awhile I handled Moon tugs on the Luna run. Then I banged swamp cabs around Venus for six years before I got into this crazy game."

"And just how was that?"

"My great-grandfather Challis was a private dick in a place they called California. In Los Angeles, on the prequake coast, way back in the 1970's when they still chased hoods in cars with gasoline engines." I grinned. "In a way, I guess you could say the detective business runs in my blood."

"Keep talking," she said—and I did.

"I'm not proud. I'll take any job that'll pay the rent on this Martian flytrap." I gave her a hard glare. "But I'm no

8

phony. I play a straight game for my clients. I'm licensed to pack a .38 notrocharge fingergrip Colt-Wesson under my coat, and I've had to use it more than a few times in my somewhat checkered career. I don't gamble because the one time I tried it in New Vegas I lost everything but my pivot tooth. My lusts are twofold: hard drink and soft women. I'm a sucker for a sob story, but I'm nobody's patsy." I slapped the desk. "Satisfied?"

I guess she was, because she lowered the .25 and let out a triple sigh. "We need help, Mr. Space. We need *your* help."

"Who's we?" I asked, easing back in my chair and stowing my wallet. The sandworm had beat my time and was already halfway down the wall. I wished him luck.

"My name is Esma Pitcarn Umani. I was adopted as a child on Venus. My Earthfather is Dr. Emmanual Quantas Umani."

"The scientific gink?"

"Yes," she said, nodding one of her heads. "He's waiting outside. We wish to employ you."

"Well, I'm for hire, sister. Two hundred solarcredits a day, plus expenses. If I have to work outside the System my rate doubles."

She seemed to think this was fine. "We are quite prepared to meet your fees. My father is a wealthy man."

"Then trot him in," I said.

She gave me a hesitant set of smiles and walked out to fetch papa.

I'd heard about him. A year or so back the Earthpapes did a feature spread on Dr. Umani's experiments with brain transplants. He operated a plush clinic out of Allnew York and was supposed to be a bit dotty. But brilliant.

Now he tottered in, eyes wild, weaving across the room toward my desk as his daughter tried to steady his passage.

"Sure now, an' what foine broth of a lad have we

here?" he shouted in a thick Irish brogue. He reached over the desktop and soundly thumped my shoulder. I could smell peetbog whiskey on his breath. "Are ye from Dublin, then, me boy?"

"I'm not Irish," I said.

"Neither is father," Esma assured me. "It's just his current body that's Irish."

I looked blank.

"He's presently inhabiting the body of a drunken Irishman," she explained. "In his last body he was a drunken Welshman. Father prefers colorful bodies."

I was impressed. "Guess his brain transplant gimmick works," I said.

"Oh, of course. All the bugs are out of *that*. Father's brain has been placed in any number of bodies. In fact, that's why we're here."

I rocked back in my creaking swivelchair and uncorked the Scotch, took a solid pull at the bottle, felt it burn down into the soles of my feet.

"Bless me sweet soul, but a taste of the devil's own would quench this ole man's ragin' thirst," said Dr. Umani, staring morosely at me from his bloodshot Irish eyes as I drank.

"Don't give him a drop," Esma warned. "Daddy's been imbibing all the way from Luna City."

I put away the Scotch.

Esma sat down in my best client's chair. Below her three necks she had a nearEarth body, curved like a range of Martian sandhills. Her snug skinflex outfit—which must have set papa back at least three hundred solarcredits—accented her full-thrusting bosom. She had my favored ratio of arms and legs, two each, and her thighs were plump and made for biting. I'll bite a plump thigh any time I can get one.

"Tell me what you want me to do," I said.

She began in a soft voice. "It's really quite a simple assignment. We wish you to—"

Dr. Umani, who'd been dozing on my couch, suddenly leaped up, waving his fists in the air. "Faith, an' I think they're here agin!"

Esma's three faces went pale.

Two

We all heard the same sound: a rustling patter of running feet in the hall. I swore heartily. My .38 was in the safe, where I kept it between cases—but Esma had her .25 aimed at the door.

It opened, and three hard-muscled Loonies came in, firing .45 microlaser Siddley-Armstrong heavyweights at us. I'd dived behind the desk, pulling Esma down with me. But I couldn't do anything for Dr. Umani. He took three .45 laserslugs in the chest—whap whap whap. There's no mistaking the wet slippery sound of a .45 Siddley-Armstrong doing its job.

The hall was empty by the time I'd palmed the dial safe for my loaded .38—and ole Umani was gasping out his last on the floor of my office.

"Call a priest!" sobbed the old geezer. "Let me poor tarnished soul reach the pearly gates unstained by the sins of the flesh!"

"Rot!" snapped Esma, kneeling beside him. "Stop that silly blather and pay attention. Did you bring the last one?"

Dr. Umani looked up at her, eyelids fluttering. He nodded his head weakly. "Ship . . . second locker from the back." His eyes rolled up white.

"He's going fast," I said.

"Doesn't matter," said Esma. "Just stay with him until I get back. If the Loonies return don't hesitate to destroy them."

I'd handled my share of cheap Moongoons and had no qualms about gunning down three more of them.

"Where are you going?"

"To our ship on the roof. I won't be a sec."

She was wrong. Actually she took three minutes. She returned with the inert body of a slender black man slung over her shoulder. He was dressed in striped trousers and a bright red shirt studded with gold buttons. She stretched him out alongside her father.

"Who's this?" I wanted to know.

"Never mind your questions." She brushed loose strands of hair back from two of her heads. "Keep watching for those Loonies. I've work to do."

She'd also carried in a medical bag, which she hastily opened. I'm no expert on operating equipment, but I know a brainbuzzer when I see one.

She thumbed it into life and neatly cut the top of Dr. Umani's drunken Irish head off. Then she calmly reached inside and scooped out a large egg-shaped steel cylinder. "Hold this," she said, handing it to me.

"What is it?"

"Daddy," she said. "It's Daddy, of course."

I looked down at the cylinder. It was pulsing red deep inside and was warm to my touch.

Esma was working on the black man. She buzzed open his head, took the steel cylinder from me and deftly inserted it. She used a quickstitcher to sew up the incision. "There," she said, all three of her heads wreathed in smiles. "All done."

The slender black man sat up, rubbing his skull. He grinned at me. Then he began to sing. "Poorboy work in de pits all day, shapin' and scrapin' de Luna clay, sweatin' and strainin' for de white man's pay . . ."

"Just what the hell's going on?" I demanded.

Esma knitted most of her brows and sighed. "Isn't it obvious?"

"Not to me," I said.

13

"Daddy's brain has been transplanted into the body of this authentic black jazz singer obtained from our New Old New Orleans branch. Daddy has always been fond of authentic black jazz singers."

"Workin' all day in de white man's way," sang the new Dr. Umani.

"Does he know who he is?"

"Naturally," said Esma. She put her green Venusian hand in his gnarled black one. "Daddy, you'd better tell Mr. Space all about why we wish to hire him."

"Righto, and sho'nuff," said Dr. Umani, affecting a broad early-stage Southern dialect. It was not nearly as impressive as his Irish brogue. "What we gots hyar is de last body." He thumped his chest. "An' I'm in it. No more spares hyar on Mars. De bad folk keep sendin' dose Loonies to gun dis ole man, an' iffen I don't have no more of dese hyar bodies on tap I'm cooled out for good." He looked at me with yellow-flecked eyes. "You diggo?"

"Not exactly," I said.

"My father has vital work to do here on Mars and must remain alive to do it. His enemies want him dead. So long as he lives, and continues to function, his work remains a threat to them."

"What kind of work?"

"We'd rather not go into that," she said flatly. "Our business with you is simple; we wish to hire a bodyguard. You are to accompany our next shipment of coldpac bodies out of Allnew York and guard them until they reach Bubble City here on Mars. My father's life depends on his having plenty of spares handy."

"Oh, yass. Yass, yass, oh, yass *in*-deedy!" agreed Dr. Umani.

I drummed my fingers on the desktop. Logic seemed to have vanished, and I missed it. I like to keep things logical. "Look," I said, "wouldn't it make a lot more sense

14

if you hired me as a *personal* bodyguard for your father?"

"But why?"

"To keep him from being shot again."

"Oh, he'll be shot again," Esma assured me. "My father's enemies are very persistent. They'll keep killing him off, no doubt of that. But I'll be around to see to it that Daddy's brain is re-transplanted whenever necessary."

"But won't they try and kill *you?*"

"They already have. Several times. But my particularly heavy, durable, all-weather Venusian skin resists their weapons. At least it has thus far. Of course there are many ways I *could* be destroyed and they may try one of them soon. But I'm not afraid. I just want to live long enough to see my father's experiment succeed."

"Sounds a little screwy," I muttered. "Couldn't someone else guard your father's spares enroute to Mars?"

"Deedy nossir, deedy not!" exclaimed Dr. Umani. He jigged around me, shaking his black head and laughing. "You is de one fo dis hyar job. Dere ain't nobody else dis hyar ole darkie gonna trust!"

"What father means, Mr. Space, is that we both know your record. You are a very brave, straightforward and resourceful man." Her six green eyes glowed softly. "We both feel that you are best qualified to get my father's bodies safely to Mars. *Will* you accept?"

The quaver in her tone got to me. "Okay, sister," I told her. "When do I start?"

"My father has already arranged for a ship to pick you up within the next half-hour and take you to Earth-launch. You are booked aboard flight 12, out of Bubble City for Allnew York at 0800, which just about gives you time to pack your .38 and your bottle of Scotch and take off."

"How come you were so sure I'd go?"

Her eyes softened again. "I *knew* you would, Mr. Space. Remember what you admitted about yourself—that you're a sucker for a sob story? I simply counted on the fact that you'd respond to mine."

"But like I said, I'm nobody's patsy. Let's see the color of your solarcredits."

She fished in her purse, drew out a hefty bundle and handed it over. "I'm sure this will get you started."

I whistled through my pivot tooth, counting it. "Diggo!"

"Have a good trip, Mr. Space," said Dr. Umani. He'd dropped the stage dialect and his tone was cultured and properly professorial. "You may be assured that my daughter has not overstressed our dire need. Those bodies *must* arrive undamaged in order to insure the future success of my work." He smiled gently, dark eyes gleaming. "One could almost say—the future success of mankind."

I didn't have any reply to that.

A case was a case, and I was just glad to be working again.

16

Three

I felt naked aboard the *President Agnew* on the Mars-Earth run. No civilian firearms were permitted anywhere on the ship, and my .38 had been officially impounded until touchdown. They told me I could obtain a special permit to carry it on the return run—but for this trip I was on board without a weapon. Naked against mine enemies . . .

Well, not quite. I'm trained in seventeen forms of solar combat, and can snap the trunk of a small pine tree with a double reverse dropkick, providing my shoes are on. I broke a toe trying it barefoot.

I was sitting on the aisle next to a pair of young Martians who were passionately probe-rubbing each other into a norxca state, which is the highest sexual level a Martian can achieve short of fleeking, and you can't fleek on board a spaceship. Since secondary sexual response is triggered from a Martian's outer probe there was nothing abnormal in what they were doing. But it made me nervous.

I grinned. Hell, Space, I told myself, you're getting old and crabby when a couple of oversexed Martian teeners can put you on edge. Relax. Grab some shuteye. The trip back to Mars just might be a rough one.

I was about to doze when I felt a hand on my shoulder. I spun sideways and dropped to one knee in the aisle, into a quick-combat position.

"Try that on a ship that isn't gravity-regulated and

17

you'll be banging your head on the ceiling," said a sensual voice above me. "Are you *always* this tense, Mr. Space?"

Earthgirl. In her twenties. Tall. Full-breasted—upper slopes and nipples exposed in the conventional manner of Earthdress. Her waist-length red hair was diamond dusted and smelled of English heather. She had freckles on her nose. A pleasant change of pace from the kill-crazed moon hood I was expecting to encounter. But I didn't mention Loonies to her; I just asked how she knew my name.

"Captain Shirley was kind enough to supply it," the girl said. "I told her it was an emergency, that I needed the aid of a private investigator, and she cooperated."

It figured, I thought sourly. You can't trust female space captains. They'll blab secrets to any other female on board. In my day, when I jockeyed the tubs, no female ever reached officer status. But the old days were over.

"I won't be any help," I said, sitting down again. "I'm on a case right now."

"But I only need you temporarily as an escort," she pleaded. "To accompany me from this ship to my lifeunit in Allnew York in CenPark South. Couldn't you just take some time off from whatever case you're on to escort me there?"

"I'm booked on the *President Reagan* back to Bubble City tonight," I told her.

She smiled and sat down across the aisle from me. "But the *Reagan* doesn't leave for several hours. I've often taken it and, if anything, it's usually late in launching. You'll have just *oodles* of time to take me to my unit!"

"Why do you need an escort?" I was staring at her nipples. One of them had winked at me. She was wearing sex-o-tract on them, which created that effect. Winking

18

nipples attract Earthmales nine times out of ten. She was playing all her cards face up.

"A certain dangerous individual has threatened to kill me when I get off this ship," she said.

"What certain dangerous individual?"

"His name is Thiam Ghong. From one of the dogstar planets. I found him attractive and we bedmated for a halfyear. Then I left him for a trisex pairing with an onion smuggler from Neptune. That was just before my affair with a spongeweed salesman from Ursa Major."

"Wow!" I said. "You *do* get around, lady."

She frowned. "I'm sexually potent if that's what you mean. But aren't *most* young Earthgirls these days?"

I grinned as her left nipple winked at me. "You got me there, sister," I admitted. "So what about this Ghong character?"

She sniffed, wrinkling her freckled nose. "He's just a sore loser. Thiam found out I was returning to Earth on the *Agnew* and has threatened to kill me when we land. Out of, I suppose, jealous rage. With you along he won't try anything."

"What about later?" I asked her. "What about after I'm gone?"

"I'll carry a bodyweapon. I have one in my unit. They won't allow them aboard ship. Captain Shirley's very firm about bodyweapons."

"I know," I said, patting my empty shoulder clip. "My .38's in cold storage."

"*Will* you help me, Mr. Space?" She had eyeglow on her pupils, and they gleamed like twin stars. To match the diamonds in her hair. She was some patootie.

"That's the second time in the last twenty-four hours I've been asked that question by a female in trouble," I said. "But, what the hell, I can never turn down a winking nipple."

She laughed musically, and plumped herself in my lap.

19

"My name is Nicole," she said. "And I wish to seduce you."

Our lips locked in a deeptongue that was hot enough to take paint off an Earthwall. The two Martians were still madly rubbing probes, so they didn't notice us.

Frankly, beyond this stage of the trip, I didn't notice them either.

We had no trouble at touchdown. I got my .38 back and told Nicole to wait in the ship while I scouted the outside terrain. She'd given me a complete description of Ghong, but I didn't really need it. A dogstar male is a cinch to spot in a crowd. You don't miss characters who are nine feet tall with furry orange ears.

"Okay, it's all clear," I assured the girl. "But stick close to me. If he shows, I'll deal with him."

She gave me a sensual smile, pressing her body against mine. "I'm sure you can deal with anything, Mr. Space."

I flagged an aircab and we got inside.

"Call me Sam," I said.

"But that's what I was going to ask you to call *me*," she pouted.

"You said your name was Nicole." I arched a puzzled eyebrow.

"But my middle name is Samantha, and all my pals call me Sam."

"I'm not your *pal*, sister. To me, you're Nicole. That's French, isn't it?"

"My mother was born in Paris. I spent most of my childhood there. My father was from the New West-Coast of America. He's from Sante Fe."

"That's nice," I said, nodding. This kind of small talk kept us occupied until we reached her lifeunit, facing CenPark South.

We tubed up and she palmed the door, with me covering her with my .38 in case the dogstar gent showed. I was ready for him.

What I *wasn't* ready for was the quick bodystrip she performed once we were inside. Before I could gulp twice, she was down to her natural lushly-pink self. It all happened so fast I forgot to check the unit. With all that creamy Earthflesh beckoning I dropped the .38 and went for her.

Which is when the sky dropped on me. Red and gold rockets exploded inside my skull and I tumbled forward into deep space, black and unending.

Four

Black . . .

Then red . . .

Blue . . . flaring into raw yellow.

Intense, stabbing yellow. I blinked, squinted, put up a hand to shade my eyes. I was on the floor of Nicole's lifeunit, lying in a pool of hot yellow sunlight.

Dragging myself to the window, I looked out. The shadows in CenPark told me it was too late.

I'd missed the *Reagan!*

Dr. Umani's bodies had been shipped to Mars without me, and would no doubt be hi-jacked enroute.

A lush patootie with winking nipples had played me for a patsy.

I groped for my .38, found it, checked the load. It hadn't been touched. I holstered the gun and cracked open a pack of Headrights. No detective should be without them. I placed two of the small, pea-shaped capsules against the sore side of my skull. They immediately penetrated skin and bone, going to work on my kingsize headache.

Within five seconds I was myself again.

I quick-scanned the unit. No Nicole. Which didn't surprise me; I hadn't expected her to stick around after I'd been sapped.

Obviously she worked for the same outfit who wanted Umani's experiment to fail. The old geezer was probably dead by now, with no spare bodies around for a brain switch. For all I knew, they'd killed Esma too. Everything had gone to blazes and I was the bozo to blame. I'd walked into the sap job like an Earthox to slaughter.

A thorough search revealed nothing of real worth. Apparently Nicole hadn't waited to pack because her clothes and cosmetics were still in the unit. I found the name Harmsworth on a zipcase. Otherwise, I'd drawn a blank. No pictures. No intimate personal effects. No letters. Nicole Samantha Harmsworth had flown a neat coop. She'd left nothing to tie her into any gang or organization.

I checked with the management on the way out, taking the off-chance I might be able to snag a second address for my pigeon.

"No," muttered the unit clerk, who was a scrawny number with sunken, sallow cheeks. "I'm afraid Miss Harmsworth has not seen fit to supply us with any past address." He gave me a skeletal smile. "After all, she's been with us now for twenty fullyears."

"That's not possible," I told him. "She can't be a day past twenty-five. And she told me she grew up in Paris. Are you sure you've got the right Nicole Harmsworth?"

The clerk seemed confused. He waved a skinny hand. "There is only one Harmsworth in our conapt—and her name is *Emily*. She's seventy-six. Lost her last bedmate back when she first joined us here. A skycab fell on him. Sad. Freak accident. If you'd like to leave a message for Miss Emily I'll see that she gets it. Right now she's out walking her neardogs. She always walks them this time of day."

"You been on duty here all afternoon?"

He said he had been.

"See a red-haired girl, young, pretty, leave here with maybe another guy?"

"No, it's been very quiet this period. The only person I've seen leave the unit is Miss Emily with her neardogs. Now, if you'd like to—"

23

"Is there a back door out of this joint?"

"Naturally," said the thin bird. "But it is locksealed during our dayperiods."

"Mind if I check it?"

"Follow me," he said.

We checked the back. The seal was still in place.

"Thanks, Mac," I said.

Outside, I was stumped. How had the girl and her goon slipped by old scrawny? Apparently they'd used the Harmsworth unit just to have me sapped in—but how did Nicole know the palm combination? And I wondered where Emily Harmsworth had been during all the time I was lying unconscious on the floor of her unit. Maybe she was in on the deal. But I doubted it. The facts didn't add up.

I took a skycab back to the launchport and checked with MarsLine to make certain nothing had happened to the *Reagan* enroute to Bubble City. I half-expected to be told the ship had been waylaid by pirates.

I was told something a lot more unsettling.

"I'm sorry, sir, but there is no *President Reagan* on the Earth-Mars run," declared the MarsLine rep. "I have never heard of a ship so named. The only MarsLine craft which left for Mars within the past daynight is the *President Wallace*."

"You're batso!" I snapped. "My name's Sam Space. I was booked for Bubble City. Look up my reservation."

He gave me a cool stare, then ruffled through a long passenger listing. "I have no entry on any MarsLine flight for you, Mr. Space."

I was sore. I began spitting words at him. "I don't know what kind of runaround you're feeding me, but I'm not buying it. Either you're lying or your data is all cockeyed. I was definitely booked to accompany a shipment of coldpac bodies being shipped on board the *Reagan* to Dr. Emmanual Q. Umani on Mars." I paused for breath. "Now, don't tell me you've never heard of *him!*"

24

The deskrep raised a slow eyebrow. "Why—why, yes —I've heard of Dr. Umani. Naturally. He's in all the papes."

"I don't get you."

"He was assassinated two Earthdays ago in Bubble City. Dr. Umani had been using another body, but they verified the ID through brain analysis. Three Moon criminals were apparently involved."

"Go on," I said softly.

"They also eliminated Dr. Umani's adopted daughter, a Miss Esma Umani, as well as the businessman she had contacted."

"Remember the businessman's name?"

He bit his lower lip, concentrating. "Wait . . . I have a pape here somewhere. Ah!" He brought one out; handed it to me.

I read the story and sighed. "Okay, I want you to book me on the next flight out for Mars."

"Gladly, sir."

I had a funeral to attend.

I stared down at the corpse in the plastocasket: a big, beefy guy in his middle-thirties with a scar on his right cheek and a cruel mouth. Black hair, thick eyebrows. It was a face that had taken a lot of wallops, and the nose was dented, the ears pugged.

"Too bad, Sam," I said, "you were a good man."

It was me, and no mistake. The eyes were closed but they were *my* eyes—dark and deep and as cruel as the mouth. I even recognized the cheap grey pseudsuit; I'd bought it on Uranis from a crooked little clotheshawk with six arms and no soul.

"Are you a friend of the deceased?" A soft-looking Funeral Captain was standing next to me, attempting to look properly bereaved.

"We grew up together in Old Chicago," I said. "But we've been out of touch for a while. I just read about his death in the papes. Thought I'd stop by and pay my last respects."

"How very thoughtful of you. I am sure that Mr. Space would have appreciated the gesture. How do you like him?"

"Huh?"

"Our job, I mean. The face is so *composed*, so at peace with the world. When we got him he was something of a mess."

"He looks great," I said.

The soft man nodded and clucked. "Indeed, the arrangement and presentation of the deceased is an exacting art. And one I might say which is not fully appreciated in our hurry-skurry times."

"I'll bet," I said. "Did they nail the goons who cooled him?"

The Captain shook his head sadly. "No, the assassins are still at large." He brightened. "But I *do* have the bodies of Miss Umani and her father on display. Would you care to view them?"

I'd seen enough stiffs. When you check out your own corpse it tends to depress you. "No, thanks, I'll pass on the other two."

He leaned closer to me, eyes moist and curious. "And just what is *your* name, sir. For the register, of course."

I adjusted my fake moustache. My realputty nose itched. I couldn't afford to scratch it. Not without tipping my disguise.

"Hammet," I said. "With just one 't' on the end. A lot of people spell it wrong."

"Of course," he said, writing it down carefully. "One 't' only. Are you staying on in Bubble City, Mr. Hammet? For the services?"

"Fraid not," I said.

"I think you'd enjoy them. We conduct them in rather high style."

"I'm sure you do," I said, "but I'm in kind of a rush." I grinned. "You know—our hurry-skurry times and all."

"I quite understand, sir." He nodded, fading back into the curtains.

I took one last look at poor dead Sam. And chuckled. "You sap," I said to him. "You should have kept that .38 handy between cases."

He didn't bat an eye.

He just went on looking composed.

Five

By now I knew what had happened to me, and I also knew there was only one man who could take care of the problem. The last time I'd seen him he'd been living under the Art Museum in Old Chicago.

So that's where I went.

The ancient lions flanking the entrance glared at me as I mounted the wide marble steps. In their plastoconversion they'd lost a good deal of their original majesty, but a plastolion is a lot easier to keep clean than a granite one. When I was a kid they used to get dirt in their stone pores; now they were immaculate.

At the top, a guard stopped me. "We're closed," he said. "Come back in the morning."

"I'm not here to peek at your collection," I said. "I need to see Nathan Oliver. He still live here?"

The guard gave me a grudging nod. "One floor down. He's our resident restorer. And if you ask me, he's also a crackpot."

"Nobody asked you," I snapped. "Do I see him?"

"You expected?"

"No. But he'll know me. Tell him Sam Space is here."

I waited while he went down to Oliver, patting the warm plastorump of the nearest lion. I *still* preferred granite.

When the guard returned he was pop-eyed.

"Well, what'd he say?"

"He—he says you *can't* be here!"

28

"Why not?"

"Because you're dead."

"That's beside the point," I growled. "Let me talk to him. I'll straighten things out."

I started to brush past. He took a fast step back and jerked a .22 ventrib LR beamer from his clamshell and aimed it at me. "I think you're some kind of—"

That's as far as he got. I used a flying switchover on him, chopping the .22 from his hand with my left foot while my right fist whacked the air out of his belly. Then I put him to sleep with the butt of my .38 and trotted downstairs to the lower floor, pulling off my false nose and discarding my trick ginger moustache on the way down.

Nathan Oliver went ashen when he saw me. His mouth gaped and his fat jowls quivered.

"S—S—S—S—"

He couldn't say my name.

"I'm no ghost, Nate, if that's what you're afraid of," I grinned. "It's your ole buddy, Sam. In the flesh."

He couldn't believe it. "But—the papes—the vids. They all reported your murder. Sam—you can't be alive!"

"I'm not. At least *one* of me isn't. He was gunned down by a Loonie in Bubble City."

"Then you're his twin brother."

I chuckled. "In a way you could say that. If you'll relax and get that death's-head expression off your kisser I'll fill you in on the whole smazz."

We walked into his main liferoom and Oliver slid into a deepplush pseudovelv chair, patting at his round pink cheeks with a silk hankie. In the draped yellow loungerobe he wore Nate was bell-shaped, and his naked feet seemed absurdly small against the chilled marble flooring.

"You always liked to go barefoot on the marble," I said, remembering. "You're an odd duck, Nate, yet you're

29

the only man in this world who can get me out of the jam I'm in."

"Convince me I'm not going insane," he pleaded. "Convince me that you're not some type of mad apparition sent by the cosmic Lord to plague me for my sins."

"I'm just Sam," I told him. "Or *one* of him, anyway. Some of me are alive and some of me are dead. At the moment .your world has one of each. Which is why I'm here to see you. I want out."

"Out of what?"

"Of this world. It's yours, not mine. It's the wrong one for me, Nate."

His apprehension had drained away by this stage. He put away the hankie and pushed his fat body free of the chair. "What you need is a drink. Scotch. Straight up, as I recall."

"You recall right," I said. "Yeah, I could use a touch of the creature about now."

He poured me a stiff one. It fired my insides like rocket fuel. We both sat down and I told him what had happened, making it brief. "I was hired by this triple-head from Venus to guard a shipment of spare bodies. Before I could get the job done I was waylaid by a babe with winking nips. She conned me into coming up to her unit in Allnew York where I was sapped and transferred from my world to this one."

"For what purpose?"

"They wanted me out of the picture for their own reasons. So they pulled the old parallel universe switcheroo."

Oliver nodded, double chins wobbling. He walked to the drinkcab and fixed me another Scotch. While I downed it he pondered the situation. Nate always loved to ponder situations.

"You've come to me because you think that I may be able to send you back?"

"You guessed it, Nate," I said. "When we knew each

30

other, in *my* world, you had the same job here at the Museum, restoring 20th-Century movie art, but your *hobby* involved time and space transportation. You were able to send trees and bushes into other dimensions. But I wasn't sure, in this universe, that you still had the same hobby. But you were worth a try."

"Oh, I do indeed putter about with time," he assured me. "Just last week I successfully transported a male gorilla into another universe. At least I *think* that's where he went. My indicator indicated it. With gorillas, you can't be sure of anything."

"Ever tried it with a human?"

"Not yet." His eyes gleamed in padded flesh. "You'll be my first."

We entered his workroom, the area in which he restored the cinema artifacts which made up the museum's collection. Half-restored studio backdrops, in sections, were scattered about the long workroom. Filmstar posters were everywhere, in various stages of repair. A giant rubber boulder stood in one corner, next to a rubber cliff. Both were seedy and peeling.

"I've been tinkering with this time stuff long enough to feel fairly secure in what I do," said Nate, bypassing the cinema items and leading me toward his hobbylab. "The amusing thing is, with two Sam Spaces involved, I should have immediately realized that you'd been transported." He rumbled with inner laughter, holding his vast stomach. "The joke's on old Nathan!"

"What worries me," I admitted, "is that there's bound to be an infinite number of universes in which Nathan Oliver *didn't* become a time tinkerer and I *didn't* become a private detective. What if I end up in one of those?"

"What you say is true. However, the closest ones to us in the cosmic stream are almost identical to our own. An incident or two may vary, yet the basic patterns are fixed. Since you were killed in the act of being hired for your present assignment we must assume that you are in a direct-line universe—which makes sending you back much less complicated."

Oliver's hobbylab was a mass of tubes, vats, switches and vegetation. He had plants and small trees sitting next to bushes and barrel cactus. I snagged my coat on a thornhedge.

"Over here, Sam," he directed.

Oliver took a potted petunia out of a tall, cone-shaped receptacle and waved me inside. "You take the petunia's place," he instructed me. "I was about to send it off. I'll send you instead."

"I hope you know where the hell I'm going," I said. This whole business seemed to verge on the haphazard, and I was rapidly losing faith in the fat man. If he fouled this, I could end up anywhere. And maybe the next Nathan Oliver, *if* I could find him, wouldn't know a damn thing about parallel universes. I'd be stuck for sure. I began to sweat.

"Don't worry about a thing," soothed Oliver, fingering several small dials along the side of the metal cone. "I'll have you back home in a wink." He peered intently at me. "When did you awaken in this universe? What time was it? That's important."

"Exactly 01800 hours. I checked the tree shadows. I'm never wrong on tree shadows."

"Hmmmm . . . and when were you attacked?—in your world, I mean."

I ran a slow finger along my chin. "I'll have to estimate. Let's see—we left the *Agnew* at 01600 and took a cab right out to CenPark. I'd put it at 01620."

"Splendid!" The fat tinkerer beamed. "I can put you practically spot-on. It's much tougher without a time-table."

"Say, just how did those ginks send me here in the first place? I didn't see any dimensional junk in the unit when I woke up."

"They must have used a portable rig. More sophisticated than mine. This equipment is still a bit on the cumbersome side, but it works. I'm *sure* it works."

"It damn well better," I said.

Oliver adjusted me in the cone seat, making certain I was in the right cosmic position; he attached several metal doodads to my neck and head. Then he stepped back, obviously pleased with himself. "When I activate this nodule-type activator you'll feel dizzy, then sickish. As these sensations pass, you should spin into blackness and thus out of this universe. Is all that clear?"

"Yeah, yeah. Let's get cracking. I want to find the dame that had me sapped. And maybe there's still time, in *my* world, to save doc Umani."

Nate fiddled with more dials, clucked his fat pink tongue against the roof of his mouth, then looked over at me. "Ready?"

"Right."

His eyes gleamed. His chins quivered. "Good luck, Sam!"

"Thanks, Nate. Thanks for the ride."

I got dizzy.

I got sickish.

And, with a great sparking hum, I spun into blackness.

I woke up where I'd fallen, in Nicole's unit in CenPark South. One thing was for sure: I wouldn't have to go looking for her.

Totally nude, Nicole was stretched out on the floor next to me, eyes open and staring.

She was as stiff as a Christmas turkey.

Six

Nicole was still a prime looker. They hadn't done anything to her face, and her body seemed to be unmarked.

She was lying on her back. I flipped her over and found the deep laser wound that had sliced into her flesh from neck to hips. Looked like the work of a .48 PA tri-beam rimfire Gripper—but I couldn't be sure.

Whoever had done the job had been in a big hurry because my .38 was still on the floor where I'd dropped it. I picked it up, checked the load. Okay. Now I owned *two* .38s, this one and the one under my coat from the other universe. At least I had something to show for the trip.

Nicole's murder had all the earmarks of a doublecross. Apparently whoever was after Umani had used the girl to decoy me here, then put her away for good after I was safely transported out of the scene. They didn't want to leave any witnesses around loose, and a good-looking piece of fluff always has a tendency to shoot off her mouth to the wrong Joe.

They'd made certain her mouth stayed shut.

There was nothing I could do about Nicole but the unit was worth a frisk. Last time I'd searched the wrong crackerbox. In *that* world this place belonged to a seventy-six year-old bedwidow who liked walking near-dogs in the afternoon.

I figured this time I'd get lucky and find something I could use in the case. And I did.

They'd taken Nicole's purse but they'd been in too much of a rush to grab her triptrunk. It was just to the left of the door where she'd set it down after entering the unit. Inside, neatly tucked away between a pair of scented glosex blousies, I found a faxletter addressed to Nicole S. Tubbs, sourcepunched Domehive, Saturn. I unlooped the fabcovering and read:

My dear and delightful Miss Tubbs:
Word has reached us that Dr. Umani's daughter has hired a private investigator named Space to accompany a coldpac body shipment from Earth to Mars. He must be detoured. And you have been selected for this assignment. Meet him on shipboard and arrange for him to escort you to your lifeunit. We will have an agent there to deal with him.

You will be paid well for this service.

F.

I sighed. F. had paid her well, all right, whoever he was. With a laser cut to the heart.

I had my clue. It didn't look like much but when you're in my kind of game you play the hand that's dealt you.

With any luck, F. could be my ace.

I checked out the *Reagan* by vidwire and was told it had arrived in Bubble City on schedule. Which surprised me.

Next, I piped the number Esma had given me for Dr. Umani's labunit on Mars—and was amazed to hear him answer.

"Yassah, boss. Somebody wanna gab wif dis ole black man?"

Obviously, he was still inside the jazz singer's body.

35

"Doctor, it's me, Sam Space. I thought they'd have harmed you by now."

"No, I'm quite healthy despite your ineptitude," growled Umani, reverting to his normal voice. "The cold-pac shipment arrived on time—no thanks to you—and Esma is now de-icing a hard-drinking Scottish highlander for me to occupy. I'll be slipping into him as soon as she's ready."

"That's it!"

"What's it?"

"That explains why they didn't try to destroy the shipment. I'm certain the Scottish highlander is booby-trapped. I'd stake my rep on it. Probably rigged with some type of self-destruct mechanism. No doubt they've booby-trapped the entire lot. Once your brain is placed in any one of those bodies you're a dead duck."

"I fear you may be right, Mr. Space."

"So stay inside the New Old New Orleans jazz singer until fresh bodies can be sent to you. I'll be with the next shipment. But first I've got to hop over to Saturn on a lead. Can you sit tight for awhile until I contact you?"

"Well, I would imagine so," grumped Umani. "But I *do* need to climb into a man who drinks more." Then his voice softened. "Still, I really enjoy strumming a banjo— and this is the only body I've had which can do *that*."

"Fine. Stay inside it and keep strumming. And be sure Esma sticks with you. My guess is your enemies won't try anything else at the moment. They'll be waiting for you to make a brain jump into a rigged coldpac. Which gives me some working time."

"Do you have a line on who they are?" he wanted to know.

I gulped. "Don't you *know* who's been trying to kill you?"

"I received a faxnote three Earthweeks ago demanding that I cease work on my experiment or I would not live

36

to continue it. There was no full signature. Simply an initial."

"Was that initial an 'F.'?"

"Yes, it was. How did you—"

"I don't have time to go into it now. Every minute we waste talking cuts down my advantage. I think this F. is the character we want. He murdered an Earthgirl and had me sent into another universe. That's why I missed your shipment. While I was gone he doctored the bodies."

"Well, it sho nuff soun' lak you has gots de right party," rasped Dr. Umani, slipping back into his heavy dialect.

"I'll be in touch," I promised.

"Yassah!" he declared. "An' dis hyar ole darkie be rights hyar when you wants him."

I piped off and booked a warper for Saturn.

The ride out was quick and easy.

As an Earthman, I'm proud of what our human scientists have accomplished but you can't knock the Martians and the Venusians who really got the ball rolling on warps and hyperspace jumps. And they started long before my time. Hell, even when I was a tad in Old Chicago you could get anywhere in the System in an Earthday—and it's been cut a lot since then. I took my first solo spacelark on Mercury when I was thirteen (with a little gal from Ganymede who knew how to use her nobbles)—and I was exploring Pluto at twenty.

It's a big universe. But it's been cut down to size.

I had to switch ships at Titan, taking a slower penetration shuttle to the surface of Saturn.

Domehive was a fairly large city with three or four million solar inhabitants at least, and I had my work cut out for me. Where—and *what*—was F.? For all I knew, he could be a sixteen-foot Uranian with vented mandibles or a gas-breather from the inner asteroids with transparent tentapods. Whoever he was, he was a sour number and totally ruthless. Which spells danger in anybody's universe.

I'd once tackled a case involving a pork stuffer from Proxima Centauri who'd run off with a multifem from Capella. The multifem's bedmate wanted me to trace her. When I caught up with them the pork stuffer used his pulsating lower lobes on me, and I couldn't walk for a month. A lobe job can put your knees wacky in quick order. I just hoped F. didn't have pulsating lower lobes.

I didn't have any solid contacts in Domehive, which made things tougher. No feeders or stoolies I could call on. I was running a blind trace. Still, every city has its dank underbelly, its haven for space drifters and con artists, bimbos and hoods and fringe riders—and Domehive was no exception.

The aircabbie warned me about the area. "You don't wanna go down there, mister. It ain't safe, even by domelight. And after domedark you're liable to get scrugged by a freebie."

"I can handle freebies," I told him. "And let me worry about getting scrugged."

"Oke, fella, it's no skin off my tentacles if you don't come back." He drove on in silence.

I grinned to myself. Even this tri-tentacled native of Saturn spoke the ancient cablingo of Allnew York. Cabbies were the same anywhere in the System; they all gave you plenty of free advice whether you wanted it or not.

"You can drop me here," I said.

"Sure," he said, using his grav-brake. "That'll be ten halfcreds."

I paid him and dropped out of the hovercraft. He gunned the cab back toward the heart of the city.

My destination was a tall down-at-the-heels plasto-brick pyramid in a narrow row of metal backwater units.

38

I'd chosen a joint called Igor's, where the booze was crippling, the females were squeakers and the price of your soul was up for grabs—what we Earthdicks call a Domehivedive.

I was maybe five feet inside the door when a wide-lipped squeaker ankled over and rubbed her tentacle against my leg. "Care for some hookas?" she asked.

"Not today, hon," I said. "Bush off!"

She called me a dirty name in Saturian and bushed off.

I ordered a stiff drink and began asking about a gink who signed his name F.

It took me half a domeday and fourteen dives to get the answer I was looking for. When I asked about F. this tender went purple. He was a native, and his natural color was puce. If you go purple on Saturn you're stirred up about something. I knew I was into paydirt.

"Better not ask about F."

"Why not?"

"If you want to go on living you'll stay clear of him. That's all I got to tell you."

"Oh, no it isn't." I reached over the drinkbar and grabbed him by his stalk-thin nearneck, applied pressure. "Talk," I said, "or I squeeze all the juice out of you."

"Undigit me!" he choked.

"Not till you talk." More pressure.

"Aghh . . . Kay, kay!"

I loosened a thumb.

"Roundtower. Unit ABZ," he gasped. "I heard he goes there."

I stood off and let him cool out. Then I moved in with more questions. "What's the F. stand for?"

"Can't say. We domefolk just know him by that initial. He—he does business with some of our people. You know the kind of business I mean."

"Yep," I said. "Farmed kills, private heists, nog jobs. Am I on your wave?"

39

"You're on," the tender said.

"What does F. have to do with Roundtower?"

"I've heard it's one of his branch offices. A rumor, you understand. Nobody's ever checked it."

"Well, somebody's going to now," I told him. I passed a tencredit across the drinkbar. "You keep shut on this, eh?"

"Shut," he said, nodding. His tentacles were purple at the tips, showing he was still spooked.

"Just be careful is all," he said, stroking his nearneck with a pod. "From what I hear F. don't appreciate snoops."

"Never mind about what he appreciates," I said. "Just keep your skin buttoned about my being here."

He gave me what passed for a grin on Saturn as I got out of there.

Seven

Roundtower was a gleaming alumrib cylinder of cross-stacked office units rising from one of the more prosperous sections of Domehive. It was a nonbiz day; foot traffic was sparse and only half of the quickways were in active use.

ABZ was near the top. I got a tuberlift up, stepped off onto a long metalway and found the right unit with no trouble. On nonbiz days the units were closed to the public, so I had to jimmy the door. At least I wouldn't have to worry about customers.

It was black inside with the domewindows zipped but I had a flashpointer with me and used that to case the unit.

F.'s office was richly furnished in a neo-classic skin motif. The desk was topped in Earthzebra. The couch was covered in Martian zeebskin, and the high-backed chairs shimmered hypnotically, upholstered in cured Venusian rainbeast. I figured if F. knew what I was up to at the moment he'd enjoy adding my skin to the collection.

I still had no idea what the unit contained, or what type of business F. conducted. Everything was neat and tidy, with no visible clues as to what game F. played here. The desk was my best bet.

It was big, with several flowdrawers on each side. I placed my flash on the zebra-striped desktop and leaned to jimmy the first drawer.

But I didn't finish—because suddenly my flash was

knocked to the floor and extinguished.

I spun around, blind, and got caught along the jaw with a blow that nearly snapped my head off. I was on my knees, half-stunned, when I got kicked in the stomach, hard. Normally, this would have had me retching and in no condition to retaliate but using the Pluto deep-breathe method I had drum-tightened my abdominal muscles and the kick was not effective. I lashed out with stiffened fingers and connected with flesh. A startled human grunt told me we were on even terms: my enemy was an Earthling.

Could this be F.—striking at me from the darkness? If so, why hadn't he used a weapon? What did he expect to gain out of keeping me alive? These questions whipped through my mind as I felt a steel-hard arm encircle my neck and jerk me savagely backward into the wall.

I countered with a kneedip half-reverse twist he hadn't been expecting which allowed me to skin free of the armhold.

Time to take the offensive!

I pivoted and sliced my left knee into his body at what I judged to be gut level, heard another loud grunt of pain, and was in the midst of a follow-up hammerkick when he used a Mercury fadeaway on me. My foot jabbed empty air.

So. This boy was a pro, who seemed to know as much about specialized solar combat as I did. Which was plenty.

We circled each other slowly in the darkness. I'd lost my .38 during the scuffle, so I was now depending on my trained hands and feet. They were, however, as deadly as any .38 in the System!

More wary circling. My eyes, having adjusted to the pitch, picked out a bulky moving form, black against black—and I charged in to deliver a fierce Uranian elbow slash that rocked my opponent.

We grappled, close-quarter style. I felt tough human

fingers close around my throat, cutting off my air. I stiff-palmed his wrists, breaking the stranglehold.

Now I was desperate; this character could put me away if I didn't act fast.

It wasn't easy. He used a Betelgeux downchop and my left arm went dead! I back-stepped abruptly away from a hard right looper which could have decked me.

I put the desk between us to give my arm time to renew itself. The dark form feinted left but I knew the gambit and avoided contact. The blood was beginning to sing in my crippled arm; I flexed my elbow, my fingers.

A solidly-thrown punch caught me under the ribs as I came around the desk, both my arms in working condition again. I jabbed a quick left elbow into his chest and topped it with a crossover right to the head.

I had him! He was off-balance when I slammed a one-two combination into him, my right fist connecting solidly with jawbone. My enemy fell abruptly away from me. He was down, finished.

The battle was over.

Breathing raggedly, exhausted from the killing encounter, I fumbled in the dark for my flash, found it and activated the cone—picking up my .38 in the process.

Had I captured the infamous Mr. F.? I was anxious to see what he looked like, beyond being human.

The bright cone of the flash cut through the pitch and steadied on a face. I let out a yowl. I swore. I ground my teeth.

It wasn't F.

It was a beefy guy in a cheap gray pseudsuit with black hair, thick eyebrows and a cruel mouth.

I knew him.

His name was Samuel Space.

When he came to I had the wallglows on. Sam sat up, blinking, and I grinned at the shock and confusion chasing each other across his ugly mug.

43

He squinted, trying to get me into clear focus. "Who—who the hell are you?"

I kept grinning. "I'm you, Sam, and you're me. Or, to put it another way, I'm me and you're you but we're both us."

"I must be going off my nog," he said, rubbing his sore jaw. "I tagged you for F."

"Same here," I said. "I guess we both got a surprise. Uh . . . sorry about the jaw." I helped him up.

"Forget it," he grunted. "I'll take a lot worse before I cash in."

He still looked plenty bewildered so I tried to spell it out. "An addlepated fattie named Nathan Oliver sent me here by mistake," I told him.

"I know Oliver," said Sam. "He tinkers with alternate universes."

"Right. He was supposed to send me home from the one I'd been dumped into by some of F.'s boys. But apparently he slotted me here instead."

"Which means," Sam added, "that we're both on the same case, but in different time tracks."

"More or less," I said. "You know, they killed you in the one I just got out of. *Us*, I mean."

"When?"

"When Esma was attempting to hire us for this job. The three Loonies nailed us. I saw our body. And they cooled Esma and the doc along with us."

Sam slumped against the edge of the desk, cracked some Headrights, and let two of them go to work on his skull. "I got me a whopping headache," he said.

"Yeah, I know. Woke up with one myself after I got sapped. Did that happen to you in this universe? Did they sap you?"

"Sure," he said. "Clipped me from behind. I wasn't out long, though. I woke up when they were trying to clamp some kind of weird metal hat on me. Two hoods. Low-grade gungoonies. We mixed it up and they killed Nicole

44

accidentally. The laser charge was meant for me. I ducked and it got Nicole in the back. That threw them off-stride and they lammed. I found the faxletter from F. and traced him here."

"You didn't call Dr. Umani?"

"MarsLine told me the coldpacs arrived safely so I figured he was okay. I didn't want F. to skip Saturn before I could get to him."

I shook my head. "That was dumb, Sam. The coldpacs are rigged. Think about it. They've *gotta* be rigged. I warned Umani to stay clear of them. He was just getting ready to pop himself into a Scottish highlander but he listened to me. Thought I was you, naturally. Which I am."

Sam clapped me on the shoulder. "I always said that if I could ever split myself in half I'd be twice as effective. Thanks, ole buddy. You saved Umani for me."

"Do you know anything about F. that I don't?"

He shrugged. "Depends on what you know."

"Just that he uses the initial F.—and that this office *may* be his. I'm not even sure of that."

Sam pursed his lips. "Sorry, but that's the full extent of my own info."

"Well," I said, "let's check out the joint and see if we come up with anything."

We combed the unit together top to bottom. Nothing in the flowdrawers. Nothing in the wallcabs. A blank.

We *did* find a bottle of starhooch. Expensive stuff from Sirius. Sitting on the couch, swapping the bottle back and forth, we both began to relax.

"Did O'Malley give you a tough hustle over Nicole's body?" Sam wanted to know.

I shook my head. "Didn't report it. I just left her there in the unit, same as you. Why ask for trouble I don't need? Let Sergeant O'Malley find his own stiffs."

Sam arched a heavy black eyebrow. "That bastard is *Captain* O'Malley in this universe. Got a promotion last year for busting a green-slave racket in the horsehead nebula."

I snorted. "Must have had a fix in. He couldn't find snow in December."

We both chuckled over how dumb O'Malley was. Then I asked about the weird metal hat Sam had mentioned. "What happened to it?"

He shrugged. "I didn't know what it was, so I took it with me back to the launchport."

"*Then* what?"

"Then I stowed it in a palmlocker. Meant to check the thing out later. Like I said, it was damned weird. Had wires and stuff attached to it."

"I'm sure it's the portable universe transporter they used on me," I said. "Exactly where'd you stow it?"

"Locker zzz-one-half, lower tier," Sam told me.

"Ok," I said. "Since we have the same palmpattern I can get it open. I'd better scoot. Wish I could stay on the case with you but I'm overdue back home."

"I could always use another me if you'd care to drop back after things are settled," he said. "We could be equal partners. Space and Space."

"Thanks, but I plan to work on my own sandpile from here on. Oh, a last question."

"Which is?"

"You wouldn't happen to know what kind of experiment doc Umani is cooking up would you?"

"Nope. I just know this creep named F. is trying to stiff him before he can finish."

I sighed. "Looks like we both need to learn a lot more. And fast."

He nodded and shook my hand. "Good hunting, Sam."

"You too, Sam," I said.

He looked a little bereft as I walked out the door.

It's kind of sad, saying goodbye to yourself.

Eight

I'd been right about the metal hat. It *was* a portable dimensional transporter—and simple enough to operate. No tougher than a kid's toy.

I set the dial, clamped it on, attached some wires. Then I pressed a red stud on the side of the hat.

Zip! I was home. Hatless, naturally, since the thing automatically returned to its parent universe.

This time, at least, Nicole hadn't croaked. Nor had she taken it on the lam. In fact, when I materialized in her unit she was standing directly above me with a shocked where-the-hell-did-he-come-from expression; the glass of iced bourbon she was holding dropped from her hand.

"Didn't expect to see me again, did you, chickie?" I snarled the words. I was plenty burned at this broad.

"Look, Sam, I swear that—"

I got up and clipped her across the mouth before she could finish whatever new lie she was going to tell me. Then I grabbed the front of her blouse and gave her a good shakeup. Her lush breasts bounced like two vibra-balls in a robo game but I wasn't interested in sex at the moment.

"You either spill what you know or I mess you up a lot," I warned her. My voice was ice. "And I don't mind belting crooked dames that have me sapped and shipped out. So spill!"

"It was my ex-bedmate," she gasped, falling back on the couch. "The same one who threatened to kill me. He

47

must have been waiting for us here in the unit, and when you came in he—"

I gave her another good one across the mouth. "Try again," I snapped. "And this time start with F."

She whitened, biting her lower lip. Her eyes were fear-glazed. "How—did you know about F.?"

"You've got a faxletter from him in your triptrunk. Never mind how I found it. Just drop the lies and talk straight."

"First, may I have another drink?" she asked. "You made me spill my last one."

I nodded.

She got up and hipped into the kitchcove. I kept my eye on her.

"Are you hungry?" she asked.

"Yeah, now that you mention it, I'm starved. I could use a cheese on wheat, whole grain, hold the butter and mayonnaise, light on the salt, no pepper."

"Coming up."

I eased into the couch, keeping her in sight. My bones ached. This unscheduled universe-hopping had taken a lot out of me. And that knockdown battle I'd had with myself in Domehive sure hadn't helped any.

By the time Nicole returned with the food and drinks I'd vid-checked the *Reagan*. The coldpacs had arrived safely in Bubble City but when Dr. Umani discovered I wasn't along he'd refused to accept the shipment. Which meant the old geezer had more sense in this universe than he had in some others. Score one for the doc.

I sent him a vidfax, telling him I was coming back on the next flight with some fresh bodies.

The cheese-on-wheat was delicious, and I'd taken three hefty bites, washed down with Scotch, before I paused in mid-swallow. I felt like a chump.

When Nicole noticed me staring at the half-eaten sandwich she let out a girlish giggle.

"Funny, huh?" I said.

"You think maybe I doctored the cheese," she said. "You're furious because you didn't make *me* take the first bite. Correct?"

"Correct," I admitted sourly.

"Hunger before suspicion," she giggled.

I thrust the cheese-on-wheat at her. "Here, you finish the thing. If it's lethal we'll *both* end up stiffed."

She took a nip, chewed, swallowed and handed the rest back. "Go on, you're the starving man. I wouldn't be dumb enough to try a doublecross two times running. You'll get indigestion worrying over nothing, Sam."

I snarled, still feeling like a chump, but finished the sandwich. All I could do was believe her; she seemed to be all through with her phony act and ready to spill what she knew. I told her I was waiting to hear about F. "Who is he? Describe him."

"Can't. I've never seen him, never talked directly to him." She flushed, sipped at her bourbon. "He had something on me—dug up by one of his sneaky subworld contacts—and he used it to make me work for him. He's ruthless. I knew he'd turn what he had over to Sergeant O'Malley if I didn't cooperate in decoying you."

I let that sink in.

"What's the F. stand for?"

"I don't know that either. I'm just a small pawn in whatever cosmic game he's playing." She tossed her red hair and gave me a long, level stare. "I've told you everything I know, Sam."

"Not quite," I said. "What does F. hold against you? What dirt did his goons dig up?"

"It has nothing to do with this case," she declared with some heat. "It's personal and I don't intend to reveal it to anyone." Her sea-green eyes flashed. "If you'd like to slap me around some more then go ahead. But I've told you all I'm going to. Period."

I knew she wasn't bluffing. And I like my chickens spirited. I'd leave her pride alone.

49

"Okay, then, forget it," I said, dumping the last of the Scotch down my craw. "There's just one more thing I want from you."

"What's that?"

"Can't you guess?" This time I was leering. The cheese-on-wheat and the Scotch had put me back in a mood to dally.

And Nicole knew how to dally.

She peeled off the glosex blousie and joined me on the couch.

I peeled off everything else.

Before I left her, Nicole did remember one more thing to tell me—that F. had another branch office on Jupiter, in Whisker Town. She recalled the address on a faxcard he'd sent her.

This info made me change my plans about going directly back to Mars. It might be well worth my while to take a shot at seeing what I could find on Jupiter.

I vidfaxed Umani and told him to hold the fort until he heard from me. Warned him not to leave his unit. With Esma there I was gambling he'd be okay until I could run down this new lead.

"Be careful, Sammie," Nicole cautioned in a husky after-bed voice. She tickled my nose with one of her exposed nipples. "F. plays for keeps."

"I can handle anything he can throw at me," I said. "Trouble is my middle name."

"I don't believe you," she said.

"Okay, take a look." I showed her my license. She giggled. Then I kissed her and left.

I didn't tell her what the T. *really* stood for. My mother had exercised a wild sense of humor in naming me. Samuel T. Space.

T. for Temperance.

Nine

I was heading for the Fat Marble. That's what I call Jupiter, and that's the way the planet looks to me, coming in toward it: like a giant fat agate in the black sky. I never liked going there for a lot of reasons. For one, I figure that nobody needs twenty-five billion square miles of *anything*; the damned planet is just too big for comfort. For another, they haven't yet licked the gravity problem on Jupiter inside the domes, and I hate wearing a contra-gravbelt. But a guy like me, at about 190 Earth-pounds, would weigh close to 450 on the surface without one. And you can't hop around much at 450.

We were nearly there, so I put my belt on, snapping it into place. I guess what bugged me most about it was that the damn thing always reminded me of how pudgey I was getting around the breadbasket. I needed more exercise; maybe finding F. would provide it.

Nicole's faxcard had listed his Jupiter office address as 129 $\frac{11}{11}/\frac{1}{2}$ G-Section, Whisker Town—and that's where I headed after landfall. No use playing paddyfoot; I was going right up to F.'s and beard the lion in his den. Providing the lion was at home.

G-Section was built with future expansion in mind—a midclass nabe of massive spider units, suspended web-fashion from the central citydome. The hollow support cables doubled as tubeways. I took No. 6 and tubed up slowly toward 129 $\frac{11}{11}/\frac{1}{2}$, riding with hundreds of other commuters, a scattering of whom were Martians and

51

fellow-Earthmen. Most were native Jupes, the ambitious little mouse people who made up the bulk of the planet's citizenry.

"Are you a tourist?" one of the mice asked me. He was hatted, suited and toted a small briefbag—a respectable member of the business community.

"Nope," I said. "I'm here for other reasons."

"Having to do with enforcement, I would guess," he piped. "Otherwise, why carry a weapon?"

Being as small as he was, he could look directly up and see the holstered .38 under my coat.

"I'm a licensed detective working a case," I said.

"Oh, how Mickey!"

In Jupetalk, Mickey meant great or wonderful. It tied in with their religion; they worshipped one called the Big Mouse who came first to Earth way back in the 1920's to prepare the way for universal joy. The Mouse was supposed to have created a benevolent Earthling named Waltdisney as his human spokesman. Before the Great Quake, which knocked out the Old WestCoast in 1998, this Waltdisney had—so went the legend—built a giant shrine in honor of the Mouse. In a place they called Anaheim. That was how the sacred Mousebook told it. But I wasn't much for religious history. Worshipping some ancient rodent seemed pretty dumb to me.

"You wouldn't think what I do was so Mickey if *you* had to do it," I told him. "I hear you mousefolk don't approve of killing."

"Oh, no," he squeaked, ruffling his neck fur. "The Big Mouse would punish us if we killed. His wrath is genuine and immediate. Yet it is nonetheless exciting, in a perverse manner of speaking, to encounter a bonafide Earthdetective. Do you plan on killing anyone here?"

"Maybe," I admitted. "That depends."

"Could I watch?" the mouse asked.

"Hell, no!" I snapped, glaring down at him.

"Just inquiring," said the mouse. His whiskers twitched apologetically. "I meant no offense."

I stepped free of the tube, leaving him to continue upward. I was glad to see him go; the little devil asked too many questions. But I admired his gall. Jupes are tiny but they have plenty of gall.

According to the wallgram, F.'s office was directly ahead, just two talldoors to the left. I tensed, preparing myself for action. My plan was harsh and simple: kick my way inside, .38 in hand, and face F. square-on. If he wasn't there I'd force whoever *was* there to tell me where I could find him.

Simple.

But things didn't quite happen that way. I had my .38 out, facing the talldoor, when a swarm of police mice hit me—at least a hundred of them, squeaking furiously and clubbing my ankles with their small nearwood billies.

I dropped the .38 as pain blazed and exploded up my ankles. Any cop in the System can tell you that a billy on the ankle is damned effective. And a hundred of them, no matter how small, could put the toughest spacer out of action within seconds.

"You are officially under citystate arrest," one of the copmice informed me. He was a squad leader, with dyed neckfur indicating his rank. Several of the other mice had stunweapons aimed at me. "Do you wish to resist?"

Rubbing my sore ankles, I told them hell no I didn't wish to resist. This seemed to disappoint the squad leader; I think he would have enjoyed putting me to sleep. He reminded me of a miniature Sergeant O'Malley.

They quick-marched me back into the tube and we headed for ground level. Twenty four of the stern-eyed mice kept their weapons centered on me all the way to the bottom.

Outside the building, they had a police vancab waiting. It was a surface vehicle, and large enough to carry Earthlings.

"To enter," directed the squad leader, waving his stun-gun at me.

I climbed inside, feeling a little ridiculous, and the two-dozen armed mice joined me for the trip to HQ. The squad leader sat next to the driver, holding my .38 on his lap in a giant zipsack. The gun was larger than he was, which made things a bit awkward for him.

Mouse Headquarters was an odd jumble of flat white windowless cubes in a dizzying variety of sizes. If you were a giraffehead from Oberon they had a very tall cube for you; if you were round and squat, as were the slugbellies from Callisto, they had a wide cube to fit; if you were Earthsize they used yet another special cube designed for humans.

I was impressed.

They took away my contra-gravbelt after I was seated. My body suddenly seemed gross and massive. Under the crushing pull of Jupiter's raw gravity it took immense effort simply to raise my arm.

The mouse in charge of questioning sat down at a tiny desk facing me. The desk was on a raised platform in line with my nose.

"I'm Police Inspector McFarlin," he told me. He was solemn and gray, with multi-dyed neckfur; he wore thick rimless glasses just above his whiskers. "You are guilty of a very serious crime, Mr. Space."

He prodded my ID papers with a large pair of forceps.

"How can I be guilty of anything? I haven't been given a hearing."

"Unnecessary," he piped. "We dispense with hearings when we have mouse-eye evidence, as in this case. You are clearly guilty of attempted assault with a lethal weapon, combined with potential forced entry." He removed his eyeglasses with a brown paw and regarded me with watery eyes. "Why are you Earth people so violent?"

He didn't expect an answer to that and I didn't have one for him. Instead, I asked him a question that had been rankling me. "How did you know I'd be there? Did that nosy bizmouse I talked to in the tube turn in a police alarm?"

"No, he did not," said McFarlin. "You needn't concern yourself with who tipped us. Suffice to say that we had prior warning that you were on your way to the site. We were, of course, helpless in a legal sense until you pulled out your weapon. This gave us full authority to move in and arrest you."

I wondered if Nicole had set me up. Again. It didn't scan otherwise. No one else knew the address I was headed for. Had she given me another con? I wasn't sure. But I'd find out.

"As to my weapon," I declared. "I have an indate solar permit to carry my .38 and it's legal anywhere in the System. I had good reason to believe that a dangerous criminal—a murderer—was inside that office and I felt fully justified in apprehending him by force."

"You were ill-informed, unwise and extremely impulsive in a destructive sense of the term," the mouse said coldly. "You were acting well beyond your licensed authority." He laced his paws in front of him, peering intently at me. "And just who *is* this dangerous criminal?"

"I wish I could tell you. His name begins with F."

The Inspector mouse-clucked at me. "And is that *all* you know about him?"

"I know he's ruthless. I know he tried to have me done away with and that he hired three professional Loonies to kill Dr. Emmanual Q. Umani on Mars."

"But you don't even know his last name?" The tone in the tiny voice was heavily sarcastic.

"I was about to find out when your copmice swarmed

55

all over me," I growled. "I was hitting one of his branch offices."

"That branch office, the one you were about to 'hit' with your deadly weapon in hand, belongs to one of the most respected citizens of the System."

"And who would that be?"

"Ronfoster Kane of Mercury."

"The Robot King?"

"Precisely. The entire roboforce of Pluto lies under his direct control. We wouldn't be eating Zubu eggs today were it not for Ronfoster Kane!"

"I hate Zubu eggs," I said.

"That is wholly beside the point," said McFarlin.

"Maybe F. and this Kane are in cahoots," I suggested.

"I am not familiar with the term."

"Maybe they're tied together somehow," I said. "F. sent a faxcard from Kane's office, using that address. How do you account for it?"

The mouse had reached the end of his patience. "I do not have to account for anything," he declared. "But you do, sir. To suggest that Ronfoster Kane is in any way connected with murder is simply outrageous. Why, he developed all of the robo Moonsaints—a most holy and respected group."

"Whomping up tin saints doesn't make *him* one," I snapped. "I'm going to have me a little talk with Mr. Kane."

The mouse shook his head. "Not after Minnie is through with you."

"Who's Minnie?"

"She's the key to your future, Mr. Space." The Inspector chuckled softly and stroked his neckfur. His black eyes shone behind the thick glasses. "We shall retain your weapon as a legal curiosity—as you'll have no further use for it."

"Hey, I don't think—"

But the mouse had touched a section of his desk and

the floor of the cube suddenly dropped away. "Go in peace!" he said.

I felt myself falling into darkness . . . into unconsciousness.

I woke up inside Minnie.

Ten

I was flat on my back on a hard metallic surface. Sitting up was a job without the contra-gravbelt, and it took some doing, but I made it, feeling like the fatwoman in an Earthcircus.

It was dark but the darkness was shot with eyes—countless winking lights which danced and sparkled from the walls. Sounds filled the chamber: clacking, buzzing, rasping, clicking, giant-bee sounds. And I could smell lubricants and fluids.

It was a machine, and I was in its bowels.

But what kind of machine?

Hello, there, Sam, it said. *My name is Minnie.*

Not said. Not aloud. The words were fed directly into my brain. The machine could read thoughts and answer them internally.

"Why am I in here?" I asked. "And what are you going to do with me?"

You must not speak aloud, the machine said. *Your voice is grating and unpleasant.*

Okay, I'd play Minnie's game. I mentally repeated both questions.

You are here because you broke the law. You did so because you are mentally defective. As to what I intend to do with you: I intend to cure you.

How?

I shall simply erase all aggressive impulses and

*thoughts from your mind, substituting non-aggressive
impulses and thoughts.*

A brainwash. McFarlin had sent me down here for a
lousy brainwash. A crummy little mouse with dyed neckfur was going to put my thinker on the fritz!

You see, said Minnie. *That's just what we wish to
protect you against—angry, violent thoughts regarding
Inspector McFarlin, Mr. Kane and your other neighbors
in the System. Such thoughts can only harm you and
those around you. I shall remove them.*

And she did.

Minnie's interior humming rose to a shriek. I felt metallic vibrations enter my body, my brain. Red and yellow fire seemed to bloom within my head. Colors fire-
worked before my eyes.

The vibrations diminished, died away. The fire and the
wheeling colors sparked to black inside my skull. I was
aware of the normal humming sounds of Minnie's interior.

I blinked, swallowed, ran my tongue over my dry lips.
My heart had been pounding; now the pounding slowed,
became regular. My pulse slowed, evened. I sighed.

How do you feel, Sam?

Fine, Minnie. I feel just fine.

That's nice. Isn't it nice to feel fine?

Everything is nice, I told her. *I am nice. You are nice.
It is nice to be sitting here inside you. It is nice to be visiting your friendly planet. And all mice are nice.*

I chuckled at my little rhyme.

Are you happy, Sam?

I am very happy, Minnie.

And what do you wish to do?

Nothing at all. I wish to do nothing.

But every member of the System does something.

Anything. I'll do anything. I smiled at all of Minnie's
pretty lights.

That's nice to hear, Sam. I'm going to send you back topside where you'll be gainfully employed. Won't that be nice?

Very nice, I said. *That will be very nice, Minnie. It is very nice of you to help me.*

It is my duty and my pleasure to help anyone in the System who is entrusted to me. You are a very nice man.

That's nice, I said.

And Minnie sent me topside.

I don't remember much of what happened after that until I got to Pluto. My new job on Pluto was helping the work robots find Zubu eggs.

"Look," said a large freckled scaly creature, speaking to me during my first workperiod, "I'm a Zubu and I've got a lot of problems. First of all, I don't know whether I'm a fish or whether I'm a bird—and I'm not sure what sex I am. That's for openers."

"Yes," I said. "I'm listening."

"Well, I think I'm both male *and* female which would explain the fact that I never seem to have any fun with other Zubus. That is to say, I seem to impregnate myself and fertilize my own eggs."

"Please continue," I urged.

"Fine. Next, I go to one heck of a lot of trouble hiding these eggs of mine. There's a lot of work and time involved."

"I'm sure there is," I said.

"Not to mention intensive thought and exacting locational selection. No sooner do I finally hide the last of my eggs than you people come along and go around digging them up. It's downright depressing. Believe me, it just adds to my basic insecurity and sexual maladjustment."

"I don't know what to tell you," I said to the freckled fishbird, or birdfish. "I just work here."

"It's no good talking to a work robot." The creature whistled sadly. "They're round and shiny and have metal

60

heads and lack sensitivity to Zubu problems. The minute I saw you I said to myself: he's *different*. I could see right away that you were not round and shiny and metal-headed. I figured I could really *talk* to you about my situation."

"That's very true," I told him. "I shall certainly be happy to discuss any situation with you. So long as I am allowed to do my job of uncovering Zubu eggs."

The creature looked nettled. "But that is just the thing," he said. "I want you to *stop* uncovering Zubu eggs."

"Oh, goodness me, I could never do that," I declared. "I must not let the Big Mouse down. He's depending on me to do a good job."

"I thought all you egg-grabbers worked for Ronfoster Kane, the Robot King?"

"*They* do," I said, pointing to the stooped and laboring work robots. "But I was sent here by the Big Mouse. He found a productive job for me and introduced me to a full and productive life. I am now helping feed the great masses of the System."

"And do you know what you are feeding them?" queried the disturbed creature. "I'll *tell* you what you are feeding them. You are feeding them my freckled eggs!"

I shook my head sadly. "Frankly, and in all honesty, I don't see any solution to your problem. It seems that you are supposed to hide your eggs and we are supposed to find them. That's the pattern here on Pluto and you can't alter the pattern."

"It's awfully depressing," said the freckled creature. He stood on one thin leg, then on the other. "Sometimes I feel like never hiding another egg."

"I can certainly sympathize with your plight," I told him. "Yet you have your cosmic purpose and I have my cosmic purpose. It is not up to us to question the established order. My goodness, if everyone questioned everything we'd have no order at all!"

61

"At least it's been good talking to you about it," the sad creature said, ruffling its scales. "Maybe I'm some kind of rebel. I could cause trouble for myself. I shouldn't go around questioning things."

"You really shouldn't," I agreed. "It can only lead to grief and unhappiness."

"Thanks," said the birdfish. "I'm certain I'll straighten up. I get in moods. But I'm basically not a trouble-maker."

"I'm sure you're not," I said.

He waddled off, muttering dolefully to himself.

I discovered two more freckled Zubu eggs and added them to my day's catch.

Pluto is 3,670 million miles from the Sun and it tends to get chilly. But I didn't mind. The Big Mouse was generous in finding me such a nice place to work. I was allowed to eat three Zubu eggs per workperiod, and they were certainly delicious. I slept in a nice wooden box called a coffin, built for me by a work robot—and I was provided with some nice reading material. I read it all through my nonworkperiods and enjoyed it a lot. Some of it was called *The Three Little Pigs*. Other reading materials I especially liked were *Goofy Goes to Market* and *Donald's Big Birthday Party*.

I read them over and over.

I don't recall exactly how long I uncovered Zubu eggs. But I do recall the day my nice friend Nicole showed up on Pluto with a metal box under her arm.

"Hello there, Nicole. It is surely nice to see you. I hope you are well. Isn't it lovely up here on Pluto?"

"They've brainwashed you, Sam," she told me.

"What is brainwashed?" I asked her.

"Never mind, just do as I say." She put the metal box on the ground. Then she attached some nice wires to my head. They led back to the box.

"Now sit very still and don't talk," she said.

"I have to go to work soon," I told her with a smile. "There are a lot of new Zubu eggs to uncover."

"Not for you," she said. "Not anymore."

Before I could ask her what she meant she did something to the box.

I felt a vast humming inside my skull.

Vibrations.

Red and yellow fire.

Whirling colors.

I blinked. My heart slowed. I swallowed.

"Are you okay, Sam?"

"Yeah, I'm okay," I said. "Thanks to you, sweetheart. Those mice had me daffy. How'd you find me?"

"F.'s gungoons broke in after you left," she said. "They tortured me into telling them where you'd gone."

So I'd been right about Nicole's tipping the address.

"Go on," I said.

"I finally got away from them and took off for Jupiter. Found out you'd been sent here for breaking the law. The rest was easy. I borrowed this clearbrain juicer from a supersolar agent I know on Ganymede and brought it here to Pluto."

"How could you be sure it would work?"

"It's designed to clear away any artificially imposed brainwaves of whatever type or origin. Supersolar agents are always having to unscramble brains."

I nodded. "I buy your story. Let's head back to Bubble City. I'm worried about what might have happened to Dr. Umani and his daughter."

"It's already happened, Sam. That's why I rushed here to unscramble you." She gave me a look of desperation. "They've kidnapped Esmal"

63

Eleven

On the Mars run out to Bubble City Nicole explained things.

She had contacted Dr. Umani after she'd talked to the police mice on Jupiter, telling him I'd been exiled to Pluto. He said that was too bad because his enemies had just captured Esma and that it would be a good thing if I could go looking for her and that he couldn't leave his experiment in its current vital stage of near-completion.

"Doesn't the old man *care* if his daughter is kidnapped?" I asked.

"Oh, yes, he seemed very distraught," Nicole admitted. "But he kept talking about sticking close to the nitty gritty."

"I intend to find out what the hell's going on in that lab of his," I said. "I don't like playing a high-stakes game in the dark."

Dr. Umani met us outside the door of his lab on the outskirts of Bubble City. It was something of a shock, seeing him again, since the body he now inhabited was that of a giraffehead from Oberon.

"Glad to see you alive and well, Mr. Space," he said, extending a polished hoof. I shook it.

"Any news of Esma?" I asked.

"I'm really not expecting any at the moment. Did you bring back some bodies for me?" He swung his long-necked head to and fro nervously six feet above us. I had

64

to look almost straight up in order to converse with him.

"We didn't have time to round up any," put in Nicole.

"Yeah, I wanted to get here fast," I said.

"I really prefer Earthbodies," he nodded, flaring his wet black nostrils and snorting. "But after my authentic jazz singer's body suffered extensive damage I was forced to take pot luck, as it were, on another. This giraffehead was the best I could scare up here on Mars, and I had to pay a premium to get him. My first cousin Verlag made the brain switch but I think he got me in sideways. I can only see out of one eye."

"I notice you're favoring your left," I said.

"And these hoofs don't help any," he added. "Difficult to get scientific things done with a hoof, I'll tell you."

"I can imagine." I peered up at him. "Nicole told me you were in the final stage of your experiment."

"Near-final," he corrected me.

"Okay—but it's almost done, huh?"

"Let us say that I can see daylight at the end of the tunnel." He lowered his horned head and began to nibble on my hat. It was a snapbrim from Earth, an old nostalgic antique hat from the 1930's that I sometimes wore on a case.

"Hey, lay off that!" I yelled, pulling back.

He gave me a sad left eye. "Sorry. But I seem to favor hats in this body. Eating hats is apparently one of the things that a giraffehead does."

"Not *this* hat," I said. "This hat can't be replaced. It's historic." I looked it over; there was a tiny nip out of the band.

Nicole was getting nervous. She tugged at my sleeve. "Listen, Sam—shouldn't you be going after Esma?"

"That's actually the job of the Solarpolice," I said. "In fact, maybe they've found her by now."

"No, no, no . . ." Dr. Umani swayed his neck to and fro. "That wouldn't be possible, since I didn't report her kidnap."

"Why not?" I wanted to know.

"It is imperative that total secrecy be maintained with regard to my experiment. I cannot risk a passle of solar snoops buzzing around me day and night."

"I think you're a sap," I told him bluntly. "Your daughter's safety should come ahead of some lousy experiment."

Umani's dustmop tail flicked against his rump. "Don't you think I have deep affection for Esma?"

"You haven't shown any."

"If my work succeeds," he said in a solemn tone, "then the whole System may be saved, not just my daughter. I can't risk failure. Esma would be the first to understand."

"It's high time I find out for myself what's in that lab," I declared, moving toward the entrance door.

"Not yet!" Dr. Umani trotted to the door, lowering his head toward me, horns at the ready. "I cannot allow even you, Mr. Space, to enter my work quarters at this stage."

"Then tell me the score," I said. "Fill me in on exactly what you're doing and who these enemies of yours really are. If you don't I'm off the case. As of now."

"Oh, Sam, you wouldn't abandon Esma," cried Nicole. "You're not that kind of heel."

"Indeed he isn't," Umani assured her. "Mr. Space would never abandon my daughter in her hour of need."

I was running a bluff, and he knew it. I was trying to pressure him for info and he wasn't falling for it.

"You'll be told everything about my experiment in due order," said Umani, his big liquid eyes shaded by heavy lashes. "I must ask you to trust me."

"What other choice do I have?" I asked, ducking as he took another swipe at my hat. I took it off and stuffed it under my shirt. No use tempting him beyond his control. "Is there anything you *can* tell me at the moment?"

"There surely is," he said. "I can tell you that Ronfoster Kane, the Robot King, is involved in this savage business."

"How do you know he is?"

"I heard one of the kidnappers mutter his name. A slip, I'm certain, yet it was enough to convince me that Kane is behind my daughter's abduction."

I nodded. "This verifies what I already suspected. In fact, Kane could be F.—using that initial as cover: I began to hook the two of them together when that cop-mouse on Jupiter told me F.'s office belonged to Kane. He may have bought off the mice, since they refused to listen to my logic in linking F. with Kane."

"If my guess is correct," said Umani, "he has Esma imprisoned in his castle fortress on Mercury. Kane has a fire dragon guarding the place, a short-tempered brute, I'm told. But he sleeps a lot."

"Kane?"

"No, the fire dragon. He's reportedly sluggish and inclined to snooze until riled. Once riled, he is a handful to deal with."

"I'll keep that in mind," I said.

"I shall look after Nicole while you're gone," promised Umani.

"Good," I said. "I wouldn't want the goons to go over her again. She was tortured, you know."

"Oh, my!" Umani trotted close to the girl and swung his long-necked head down to stare at her with his good left eye. "What did they do to you, dear?"

"For one thing," she told him, "they tweaked my tummy with fern needles. And that *hurts!*"

She showed us her tummy and the tweak marks.

"Then they raped me," she said matter-of-factly.

"How terrible!" exclaimed Dr. Umani.

"Not really," she said. "I've been raped lots of times. It's not so bad once you get used to it."

"I'd better cut out," I announced.

"Not before I tell you the terms," Umani protested.

"What terms?"

"Upon which the kidnap was based. Every kidnap has terms. You get them as part of the package."

"Shoot," I said.

"I'd best re-construct the scene," said Umani. He sat down in front of the lab door on his haunches and folded his two front hooves. His left eye regarded me with immense sadness. It was the long lashes which gave that effect. Every giraffehead looks sad. "We were obtaining a pre-work snack in the YumYum section of the city," he related. "Myself, in the body of the splendid old banjo-strumming jazz singer, my daughter Esma and my first cousin Verlag. We had ordered a light repast of stippled gork's milk and toasted nobbins and were seated at a Yumtable about to eat when the side of the building melted."

"What material?" I wanted to know.

"You mean the buildings?"

"Yeah, what was it made of?"

"It was a claybrick and limecrix affair with a nearstone base so far as I could determine."

"Then they must have used a .20-40 Emerson heavy-frame swing-cylinder de-energizer," I said.

"Quite possibly," declared Umani, a note of irritation evident in his voice. "I'm no weapons expert, Mr. Space. Might I continue?"

"By all means."

"When the wall melted I immediately sensed that *we* were the targets. Therefore, I threw myself across Esma in order to shield her from impending danger. Three muscled Loonies entered the Yumroom."

"Same ones who put your drunken Irish body out of commish?"

"The very same. They charged in and struck Verlag brutally to the floor—which subsequently worsened his liver condition—filled my authentic jazz singer's body

68

with nitroballs and made off with Esma, muttering Kane's name as they did so."

"What about the kidnap terms?"

Umani snorted, nostrils distended. "I'm getting to that."

"He's doing his best, Sam," said Nicole.

"The kidnap terms were clearly printed on a faxcard which they left on the Yumtable."

"Still have it?"

"No, it self-destructed. But I memorized the terms. I have a *talent* for that sort of thing. Helps me in my work when I have to remember complex formulas."

"What about the terms?"

"Oh, yes. I shall quote them." Dr. Umani's horns lifted and his pink rubbery lips pursed. "The card began: 'To Whom It May Concern.' Then it continued: 'We have once again attempted to wipe out Dr. E. Q. Umani. But if, by happenstance, his brain is transferred to yet another body and he lives he must heed our warning in order to keep his daughter alive. The Umani Experiment must cease. It must not be brought to completion. If it is the girl will be done away with. Painfully. If, within the next Marsperiod, this experiment has indeed been abandoned and the lab destroyed, then the girl will be allowed to live, although she will be retained until certain plans have come to fruition.' And that was the end of it."

"What plans?" I wanted to know.

"Never mind," Umani snorted. "The point is, I *must* continue my experiment. And *you* must bring back Esma. Her life depends on you."

"What is Kane's connection with your work?" I asked. "And what—"

He cut me off with a raised hoof. "No more questions, Mr. Space. Verlag is waiting for me in the lab. I must trot. Come, my dear." He nodded his head at Nicole. "I'll show you your quarters."

"See you later, Sam," Nicole said.

Umani gave me a parting smile. Big yellow teeth in black gums.

I never liked to watch a giraffehead smile.

Twelve

"You seen Gimpy around?"

I was doing the asking. The dogface to whom I'd directed my question was big and shaggy and built like the side of a bank. His name was Ham Bodeen and he never said three words when he could say two and never said two when one would get the job done.

Now he said, "Naw."

"When was he in last?"

"Week ago," said Ham.

"Alone?"

"Nope."

"Who was with him?"

"The usual."

He meant TeTe, Gimpy's hanger. Gimpy Hovel was too dumb and too ugly to latch onto anyone better than TeTe, an ex-goongirl whose best days—and nights—were behind her.

"So she still flops with him, eh?"

"Still."

"Where?"

"Hard to say."

I slipped him a fiver. "Any easier now?"

We were at a table in one of the rougher dendives on Luna, and in a place like this it's better to keep your credits out of sight. That's why I passed him the fiver under the table. His big hardskinned paw folded over it

71

and his dog-bright eyes gave a flicker. He was going to tell me more.

"Old Colony," he said. "Second fleahut from the crossing off Blackcrater Road. You might try it."

"I just might," I said.

Blackcrater Road had been slashed into the lunar surface back in the days when the first Moon colony was established, and it was in lousy shape now, tough to negotiate even in a sandcar.

The area was stark and deserted, a fetid backwash of cracked domebuildings and occasional fleahuts—which had housed the Moonworkers when the colony had still been operational.

The sandcar I'd rented was nearly as used up as the area around it; the vehicle wouldn't respond to more than halfpower and its engine labored to propel it over the pitted, rock-strewn road. I was beginning to heartily curse its poor performance when the Gimp's fleahut popped into view over a sandrise.

It was where Bodeen said it would be, just one hut past the crossing. I spotted Hovel's dented sandbike, meaning he was inside. With TeTe, no doubt.

I cut power and climbed out of my machine.

The fleahut's slidedoor was unsealed, and I didn't bother to knock. The Gimp was an old pal of mine.

He was there all right but he wasn't in any condition to say hello. The strong odor of Moonjuice hit me like a fist as I stepped inside. Hovel was on a fraying, half-sagged plastocot near the wall, flopped on his back, arms flung out, mouth open, breathing harshly through his fleshy nose.

He was juiced to the eyeballs.

"Who the freeb are you?" demanded TeTe. She was at the hut's table with a drink in front of her, a skinny little blueblonde in a faded slackbag. The bag had holes at both elbows. From the anger in her eyes I could see she was still sober enough to talk.

"If it matters to you, sister, my name is Space." I nodded toward the Gimp. "Wake him up fast and pour some hot Earthcoffee into him. I need the bum."

"Don't try and give me orders, you—"

I whacked her once and she shut up, knowing I'd do it again. "You heard me. Move it!"

She hauled Gimpy into a sitting position, yelling at him to wake up, that there was some kind of nut here to see him.

"Huh, huh, huh," he sniffled. "Whosa matter?"

I walked over and grabbed a handful of shirtfront, pulling him half off the cot. "Wake up, Hovel! You've got what I need and you're going to give it to me. C'mon, *on* your feet."

I jerked him up. He swayed there, blinking me into focus. "Sam . . . Sam, ole pal."

"Yeah," I said, smacking him hard with the flat of one hand while I held him up with the other. "It's your ole pal, here to collect a debt."

"You're outa luck, Space," declared TeTe sourly, beginning to fix the hot java, "The Gimp here can't pay nobody nothing on no debt. He's flat."

"I saved this bum's life once on Deimos. A shagbeast had him by the ass. I gunned the shag. And for that he owes me. But I don't want what he hasn't got. I'm not after credits."

"Then what *are* you after?" She gave me a curious look in mid-gesture, the coffeepot in her hand.

"Info." I shook Hovel until his eyes jiggered; then I smacked him again. It didn't help much.

He slumped onto a nearstool by the table, groaning, holding his head in both hands.

"Get that coffee into him," I said. "Now!"

"Gimme two seconds willya?" TeTe kept fiddling with the ancient Moonstove. The pot bubbled and hissed.

73

"Now, I said!"

"Okay, okay," she said, carrying over the steaming pot. She got out a cup, filled it.

I took the stuff to Hovel, made him drink it black. He coughed and sputtered but he got it down.

"More," I directed. "He's still half out and I want him talking."

We continued this routine for maybe five cups. Then I grabbed him by the hair and yanked his head back. "I need some info, Gimpy. You understand me?"

"Sure . . . sure, Sam . . . Jus lemme . . . pull myself together. My head hurts."

I stood above him while he fought the juice. He'd had plenty but the hot java plus my wakeup treatment had brought him to the surface again.

"You know every goongun for hire on Luna," I said. "I need to find out about three particular ones."

"Which . . . which ones, Sam?"

Hovel had smuggled illegal tobacco plants for awhile; then he'd gone into black-market soapweed. He'd even had a stable of goongirls until they gave him the ditch. He knew what I had to find out.

"Three Loonies who work for Kane. They tried for a hit on ole doc Umani twice in Bubble City. On the last trip they grabbed his daughter. I want names. And I want to know where to find them."

Hovel rubbed his forehead. "You wanta know a lot, Sam. I could get in some big trouble playin' goonstool for you."

My eyes narrowed and I leaned on the table, lowering my face to line up with his. I looked mean and I was. "Talk to me or I give you a lot more than Moon trouble. I'll toss you into that sandcar and haul you back to Earth and turn you over to O'Malley. He's got big fists and a long memory." I gave him my wolf's grin. "O'Malley would lick his chops over you."

"Aw, Sam . . . you wouldn't do that to a pal?"

74

"Not if you sing for me I won't."

He groaned, sweating, hands shaking. He was caught and he knew it; there was nothing he could do but give me what I wanted.

TeTe watched us from the far corner of the hut. She crouched there, out of the action, wanting no part of a guy like me.

"I—I think I know the goons you're after," said Gimpy. "They're on Kane's paysheet I know. Heard 'em braggin' about it. He uses 'em from time to time on hard-knuckle jobs. They don't mind tellin' about it neither. They figure it's kind of an honor, doin' knuck jobs for the Robot King."

"Names," I prodded.

"I just know 'em by their nicks," whined Hovel. "One's called Fruit, cuz he likes eatin' all kinds of it. He especially loves them big cherry plums from Venus. Usually he's got cherry plum stains all over his shirt."

"Snap it up," I growled. "Who're the others?"

The Gimp scrubbed at his cheek. He was nervous but he was talking and that's what mattered.

"The second one's called Spider. He's shaped that way. Kinda lumpy and hairy. Third's called Kid Smiley, cuz he never does. Smile, I mean. The nick's kind of an irony, see?"

"I get it," I said. "Where do they stash?"

His face glistened with fear sweat. "I . . . I'm not sure I can—"

I doubled my fist. Hovel flinched away from me. "Wait. Wait a sec. I can remember. Yeah, I *do* remember."

"You're lucky to have such a good memory," I grinned. "Saves you getting your nose busted."

He returned my grin with a sour, uncertain one of his own. "Try the Jet Juicer in Rim City. Kane's goons go there for spinkas."

"How are they stocked?"

75

"Fruit carries a custom .30-70 quickfire sleevebreech Rugby-Powell with him. Spider's off the iron; he packs a skinner in his boot. Long blade. Kid Smiley favors a .20-40 Vickers stemline Special with automatic side load. And they all know what to do with what they carry. They're bad news, Sam."

"They used .45 microlaser Siddley-Armstrong heavy-weights for the first hit in Bubble City," I said.

"That's off-Luna equipment. Here they stick with the lighter stuff. But they can handle just about anything. Kane's a careful picker."

"What else should I know?"

"Nothin'—except when you show don't mention my name. I'm dead if any of them Loonies ever gets the idea I'd finger 'em."

"You worry too much," I said, handing him a cup. "Drink up, Gimp."

He backhanded the empty coffeecup away from him, grabbed a bottle of Moonjuice and poured. "That coffee'll rot my gut," he said.

I turned to TeTe. She hadn't moved. "You need a new man, sister. This one's a juicehead who's all out of future."

She didn't say anything, just glared at me from the corner.

Gimpy was still shaking when I went for the sandcar.

Thirteen

I was never any good at spinkas. It's strictly a Moon game utilizing spinkas balls, the big fat round kind, and the idea is to catch your opponent off-guard and knock him down with a solidly-pitched ball to the chest. Head and stomach shots are fouls. Three knockdowns and you win a round.

Under the Moon's lesser gravity such a game is possible; on Earth it would be too exhausting. Even here, you need to have the build for it.

Loonies come light and dark, tall or short, bearded or clean-shaven—but they all have one thing in common: they are muscled like pro wrestlers. Spinkas lets them work off steam between jobs.

When I got to the Jet Juicer in Rim City a game was in progress. The wet solid *thwack* of a spinkas ball to the chest and a gruff burst of lewd shouting told me somebody had connected.

I beamed in on three beefy types tossing the balls at each other near the back of the room.

Ordering a Venus fizz, I asked the divekeep about the trio. "I'm looking for Fruit, Spider and Kid Smiley," I said. "Would that be them?"

"It sure would, buddy." The keep set my fizz on the drinkbar. He'd lost an arm on the jets and had never bothered to replace it. It was his badge of service. He waved the stump at the three gungoonies. "They don't like strangers bustin' into their game. If I was you, I'd stay clear of them right now."

"But you're not me," I said, downing the fizz in three quick swallows. It was liquid fire, and I needed some heat for what I was going to do.

I walked over to the short, lumpy guy—who had to be Spider—and grabbed his spinkas before he could do anything about it. Then I swung around and whacked the ball, full-tilt, into the chest of the sour-faced Loonie who nicked as Kid Smiley. He wasn't expecting a play like this and went down hard on his butt. The third goon, Fruit—with plum stains all over his shirt—made a snake lunge toward his belt for what I guessed as his custom .30-70 quickfire sleevebreech Rugby-Powell but I had my .38 out and pointed before he could make the draw.

I disarmed all three of them. Spider tried for the skinner in his boot but I barrel-chopped it out of his hand. He looked dismayed, sucking at a cut knuckle.

The divekeep was watching the action with a hanging jaw; he'd never seen these boys roughed before.

I nodded toward the back rooms. "Start walking."

"Wait, bo, we—" began Fruit.

"Hop it!" I rib-tapped him with the .38, which he didn't appreciate. And he walked. They all walked.

A short halflit passageway led into a back gamble-room. I herded them inside, kicked the door shut.

Then I waited for their angry questions.

"What kinda heist is this?" from Spider.

"Why the fancy play?" from Kid Smiley.

"Who are you anyway?" from Fruit.

I gave them my coldest grin. "I'm here from Kane. He's not very happy with the way you three creeps handled the girl's kidnap."

"How come he isn't?" demanded Spider. He was dark and hunched and hairy. "We done a good clean job!"

"He wants to know where you've taken her."

78

"Just where he told us to," put in Fruit. "To the South Tower on Merc. What's his gripe?"

"Kane likes smooth work. You three are fumblers. You let a cheap private op trace you here."

"What cheap private op?" Kid Smiley wanted to know. He was about my size and height with heavy shoulders and long arms.

"*This* one," I said, pulling off my trick moustache and triggering the .38 three times.

They went down like axed trees—and I counted the System lucky to be rid of three murdering gungoons. I felt virtuous and cheerfully heroic. If Kane wanted more of his dirty work done on Mars he'd have to hire some new blood.

I wasn't finished with the job here yet—not until I'd taken several microsnaps of Kid Smiley. I'd packed a Poloid Zuber with me, and now I got it into action, arranging the Kid's head for side, front and rear shots.

"Okay, Kid, say cheese," I said, shooting down at his dour face. But he wasn't able to appreciate the gag.

After I had all the shots I needed I stowed the Zuber and broke out my portacarry deatomizer, the L-5-J model. It wouldn't be smart to teave three stiffs in the gambleroom when I breezed, so I let each body have a blast.

Poof! No more gungoons.

The one-armed divekeep looked startled to see me come back alone. "The boys decided to leave early," I told him. "They went out the back way."

"I'm not shedding any tears over that news," he admitted. "They scare off half my customers." He waved his stump. "Look at tonight, for instance. Not a soul in the joint."

"A little quiet," I agreed.

"What was the hassle about?" he wanted to know. "The gunwork and all."

"Minor disagreement," I said. "Nothing to worry

about. We got it all straightened out before they left."

This seemed to satisfy him. In Rim City you don't get too excited over gunwork. He gave a nod toward the game corner. "Care for a round of spinkas—me against you—on the house?"

"Nope," I said. "But thanks for the offer. Right now I've got another game to play."

My next stop was Callisto. I arrived there with a half-dozen sharp tridim shots of Kid Smiley in hand. The Zuber had done a neat job.

The plasto I showed them to agreed. "Very clear," he said, checking them under a blowup torch. "The bone structure is in sharp relief and there is excellent definition."

"Glad you like 'em," I said. "Now just make me look like that. Can do?"

"Shouldn't imagine we'll have any great problem," he said. He talked about himself as "we," but he was just one guy. His name was Zaadar and he had a solid rep as a firstclass plasto. Zaadar could make an ape look like an angel for the proper price. He was flexible. He worked legit and he worked non-legit, charging whatever the traffic would bear. We agreed on a fee and I paid him in advance. He assured me that was standard in his business.

"Lie down, please, while we prepare a hypojection," he said. Zaadar was a squint-eyed, ugly bastard, and I wondered why he didn't give himself a new face for free.

I took off my coat and stretched out on a long white medtable. I don't like needles poked into my kisser but in this case it was necessary.

"Simply relax your jaw muscles," Zaadar told me. "This won't hurt a bit."

He leaned over me and used the hypo; my skin tingled for a few seconds, then went numb.

Zaadar had mounted the six shots of the Kid over the medtable—and he studied them intently, waiting for his hypo solution to take full effect.

He pinched my cheek. I didn't react. Dead flesh.

"We're ready to begin," he said.

I couldn't say a thing; my entire face felt like a mass of alien clay. Zaadar brought that clay to life with his hands and his tools, molding and sculpting my skin and bones to the shape and likeness of the late Kid Smiley. He hummed an Old Venusian brush tune under his breath as he prodded and squeezed and kneaded. He was obviously enjoying himself.

Occasionally he's pause to check one of the photos.

"We need a bit more depth in the left cheekbone," he muttered, squinting at a mounted Zubershot. "And the eyes should be recessed another quarter-inch." He kept at it, handling my face like baker's Earthdough. "Ummm . . . that right earlobe could stand a bit of tucking in."

Finally he was done. He told me I could stand up.

I felt a bit woozy on my feet but the effects of the plasto solution were disappearing rapidly and sensation was flowing back into my skin.

"You will not experience any pain," Zaadar assured me. "Your new face should withstand any normal activity. However, for the next twelve Earthhours, until the bones harden and resettle completely, we would advise you to avoid any direct blows to the facial area."

"That's not so easy in my profession," I told him. "But I'll try and be careful. What about my *old* kisser?"

"We don't follow you?"

"I mean, can I get it back?"

"Whenever you wish," Zaadar said. "Just drop in anytime. Restoration is no problem."

"Ok," I said. "I'll do that. I'm kinda fond of me."

I checked my reflection in Zaadar's imagewall, running my fingers gingerly over the new bone structure.

It was perfect.

Deep-set eyes. Wide nose. Thin lips. Tucked-in earlobes.

I was Kid Smiley.

Fourteen

Mercury is a runt. At just over three thousand miles in diameter, it's pea-sized next to Jupiter but what it lacks in girth it makes up for in hellhot temperature, being so close to old Sol.

If you're not under a bubble on Mercury you fry like an egg. In 2020 the coolsystem failed in Domeville and ten thousand unlucky citizens were roasted. After that they put most of the heavy industrial areas underground but Domeville is still on the surface. Only it isn't called Domeville any more.

Now it's KublaKane. The Robot King bought it outright, tore down the public housing units, and built his own private fortress there, complete with dragon. Frankly, it was the dragon that worried me. I sincerely hoped to avoid him.

I'd played it dumb back in Rim City. I should have pumped Kid Smiley for info on the Kane layout before I cooled him. I had no way at this point of finding out the floor plan of the fortress. The only way to reach Esma was to run a heavy bluff. I'd mastered the low rasp which had dominated the Kid's voice, and if I said only what I *had* to and remembered to look dour I felt sure I could pass.

I was packing ample firepower: I had the Kid's gun under my travelcoat, along with my .38, and a sawed-off .60-20 Lowder-Losenby laserbeam TX, with reversable chambers, looped around my neck with the flexible barrel tip stuffed into my belt in back. A .60-20 will stop a Ganymede Gorebeast at full gallop, and those babies take some stopping.

I stripped my pressure suit in the tube leading to KublaKane and stepped toward the first guard. Like all of Kane's synthetics, he wore regulation KK black skintights with a beltweapon and bootsword.

He braced me with a hand on his weapon. "Your identity and your business."

"I work for your boss," I said in the Kid's rasping voice. "Put me on a visual scan and you'll see I'm legit."

I was ready to flash a doctored faxdisc if I had to but wearing the Kid's mug I figured I could pass a scan. If I couldn't, it was time to find out.

The black syntho adjusted his coned gatescanner and thumbed life into it. An identibeam picked me out. Gears whirred and clicked. The scanner gave its verdict: "Identity known and recognized. Smiley, Kid. Admit."

The guard took his hand off his beltweapon and nodded me through. Zaadar had done a remarkable plasto job and my new face had passed its first test.

For better or worse, I was inside Kane's kingdom.

His castle fortress was easy to spot, thrusting up from the circle of bubblehuts like a great stone fist. I marveled at the effort Kane had put into its construction. He'd even created his own mountain on which to base the castle, utilizing countless tons of Mercury crater rock. The fortress was modeled on the ancient medieval castles of Earth—which was not surprising since medieval Earth-history was Kane's hobby. A wide moat, filled with bubbling, boiling lava, encircled the huge structure and a long, winding road climbed up to a massive drawbridge.

My next problem centered on getting that drawbridge lowered since I'm not much for swimming through boiling lava.

The village below the castle was crowded with identical synthetics, moving in a flow of activity. I tensed, expecting a challenge but I was ignored. I'd passed the gatescanner which meant I was supposed to be here; thus, unless an alarm went off, none of the soldiers would question me.

I walked swiftly past the ring of bubblehuts which fringed the castle, gaining more confidence with each step. The road up was steep and pebbled, and ended at the moat's edge. Directly below me, lava hissed and bubbled.

I waited, looking dour, watching the drawbridge. A small slidepanel opened in the middle of the raised bridge and a metallic voice boomed across the moat, "Hold and state your reason for entry."

"I'm on Kane's business," I replied. "I possess custodial authority for the prisoner in the South Tower."

"Your name?"

"Smiley, Kid."

"Name of prisoner?"

"Umani, Esma."

The slidedoor closed and I waited, sweating.

I'd done some careful checking before coming to Mercury in order to make certain that Kane was not at his fortress. I'd been able to establish the fact that he was away visiting one of his robot onion farms on Venus. Secondly, I'd forged his name and official stamp on a faxdisc which gave me custody over Esma. I'm a fair hand at forgery; it's an asset in my business.

Creaking and groaning in authentic medieval fashion, the huge drawbridge began to lower itself. Down it came, slamming flush with the road edge. I walked across, radiating surly impatience.

Two of Kane's synthetics flanked the inside gate, weapons at the ready. "Your authority," demanded one of them.

I handed him the phony faxdisc. "I'm under orders to transfer the prisoner to our Deimos base," I rasped.

"Why weren't we informed beforehand?" The synthetic's eyes were beady with suspicion.

"This was a last-minute decision. That's why Kane gave me his personal disc. You can *see* that." I curled my lip, which was as close as Kid Smiley ever got to a smile. "Do you want trouble from Kane? If you do, I'll see that you get it."

That shook him. He handed back the disc and waved me past.

The heavy portcullis was raised and I entered the castle.

It was perfect to the smallest detail. Bronze Greek and Roman statues, magnificent hanging tapestries, great mounted scrolled shields, frescoed walls, wood mosaics . . . Kane had lavished a fortune here. Every item in the castle contributed to the total authenticity he demanded.

But which way was the South Tower? This is where Kid Smiley's info would have paid off. We all have lessons to learn—and I'd have to learn not to be so damn fast on the kill.

I turned to an impassive castle guard. He was outfitted in full medieval armor and carried a broadsword. I tapped on his visor. It opened.

"I'm here on Kane's business," I said. "I shall require an escort to the South Tower. Lead me there."

Simple. The armored guard clanked heavily off down a corridor without a word of argument.

So far, so good. My crazy plan might work after all.

And to hell with fire-breathing dragons!

We snake-trailed down endless stone hallways, under high and low arches, through a cobbled courtyard—in which several of Kane's castle guards were jousting with sword and lance—and climbed what must have amounted to a thousand stone steps. By the time we reached the massive iron-studded door to the South Tower room I was breathing hard and the muscles in my legs were aching. The synthetic, despite his heavy body armor, was calm and relaxed. "Here we are, at your declared destination. Do you wish me to wait for you?"

"No. Go back to your post," I told him.

His visor snapped shut and he clanked away down the twist of stone stairs.

I tried the door. It was barred. I banged on the wood with my fist. Waited. Banged again.

Was Esma alive in there?

Muffled sounds inside the room told me it was occupied. A lock rattled under a key; a heavy bolt slid back with a screech of metal. The door inched open and a bulky black synthetic filled the space, holding a belt-weapon.

"I'm here to take charge of the prisoner," I said.

"Under what authority?"

"Ronfoster Kane's personal directive." I showed him the faxdisc. He belted his weapon and allowed me to enter.

The room smelled of sweat and damp straw. Guttering candles supplied the only light. Esma was chained to the stone wall in a standing posture, totally nude, arms and legs spread. Her three heads were secured by wide metal neckbands which had been driven into the stone with spikes. Her eyes were all closed. And she'd been roughed: her body was bruised and dirt-caked.

"Release her," I ordered.

There were two other synthetics in the chamber and they hesitated.

"Unspike her! She goes with me."

The doorguard flicked his eyes, which was apparently a go-ahead, since the other two got busy on the chains.

"You're one of the three Loonies who brought her here," the doorguard said coldly. "I remember your face."

"That's right," I said.

"We were told that Kane wanted her retained in the Tower. What caused him to change plans?"

87

"That's not your worry," I rasped. "Just do your job and keep your yap shut."

He didn't like that much. His jaw tightened and his synthoeyes radiated black anger at me. But he kept his yap shut.

After a great deal of hammering the other two bozos had Esma out of her chains. She was limp in their arms as they carried her to a straw-covered bench.

I walked over and pinched several of her cheeks. Then I slapped two of her faces, hard, stinging slaps. I had to wake her up fast and get her moving.

Esma began to come round, groggily blinking her six eyes.

"C'mon, wake up, sister," I snapped. "We've got to go for a little ride, you and me."

"Just where are you taking her?" the big boy at the door wanted to know.

"Callisto," I said.

There was an ominous silence.

"That's not the right answer."

I swung toward him. "What the hell do you mean?"

"I mean you told the gate watch you were taking her to Deimos base. I know because that information was vidphoned to us here in the Tower."

"I can explain that," I said, walking over to him. When I got close enough I slammed a hard right into his stomach.

Which was a mistake. Synthetics don't *have* stomachs. Instead of doubling over he swung a crushing fist into my face. I staggered back as he reached for his belt-weapon to finish me. The other two guards were also going for their weapons.

I snapped the .38 out of my coat and knocked the pair of them down with my first two shots; my third missed the doorguard who had lunged sideways and dropped behind the table.

88

His beltgun blazed and a section of wall just above my head exploded into stone fragments.

I didn't give him a second chance to kill me; my next shot ripped into his chest and he flopped back, the gun spilling from his dead hand.

I holstered my .38 and turned to Esma. She was wide awake by now, and terrified. "Are you going to kill me? Did Kane send you to kill me?"

I knelt beside her and used my normal voice. "Listen to me, Miss Umani. I'm Sam Space, the operative you hired on Mars. I had a plasto give me this face in order to penetrate the castle. I've come to take you out of here. Are you strong enough to walk?"

"Yes, yes I think so." She gave me a warm triple smile. "Your nose is all crooked."

I felt it. She was right. The doorguard's fist had driven it cockeyed. I'd been warned by Zaadar not to get hit in the kisser. Damn! This made things worse for us.

"Forget my nose," I said. "Can you make it?"

"I'm sure I can."

"Good. Let's start—because right now we're smack in the middle of the lion's mouth and I want to get us out before the jaws close."

Fifteen

Usually, when you make a run for it, you wait until dark. But it was no use waiting for dark in this case, since Mercury's day is twice as long as its year. We'd have to chance a sunlight run.

No alarms had gone off or the place would have been swimming in guards, so we still had a fair shot at clearing the castle before anybody discovered the three stiffed synthos.

I used the heavy brass key from the doorguard's belt to lock up behind us as we left. A locked door might buy us some extra time.

Esma was wobbling, leaning on the wall for support. But she managed the steps down okay. I'd found a guardsman's silk cloak for her to wear and she looked regal in it. Esma was a beautiful example of Venusian womanhood but this wasn't the time or place for me to do anything about it.

I was reminded of the lewd Venusian joke which was taglined: "and that's why three heads are better than one." I was nine the first time I'd heard it, on Earth, and it didn't mean much back then. Now I chuckled, remembering it.

"What's funny?" Esma wanted to know.

"Nothing," I told her. "Keep moving."

On the floor of the castle, with the steps safely behind us, I realized we were lost. "How do we find our way back to the gate?"

"Didn't you just come from there?"

"Sure," I said. "But a tin soldier led me. I sent him packing."

"Ask another guard to help us. They don't know anything's wrong."

"Can't," I said. "Not with this crooked beak. They'd begin to ask questions I wouldn't be able to answer. I'll try and retrace the way back."

"Do you think you'll be able to?"

"I've gotta try. Let's go."

We began moving through more of the castle's endless arched hallways. I thought the ones we were taking seemed familiar but I couldn't be sure since each stone hallway looked just like every other one in this damned place.

"I think we're doing all right," said Esma. "I remember they took me through here. I'm sure we're headed for the gate."

She was steadier now and had regained much of her strength and spirit; tripleheads are a tough breed.

Then I spotted the courtyard just ahead.

"Our luck is holding," I told her. "I remember how to go from the courtyard."

We crossed it quickly. Most of the jousting guards had drifted off and only a half dozen remained, banging at each other with battle axes which rang like bells against the guards' bronze shields.

"They're too busy to notice us," whispered Esma's nearest head.

She was right. We made it across without incident.

"I'm starved," sighed Esma, as we neared the great dining hall of the castle. "Couldn't we take a detour in there?"

"I could use some grub myself," I said.

The dining hall was deserted. The long table was stocked with bowls of ripe, tempting fruit. While Esma packed apples and pears into the flared pockets of her cape I filled two fat crystal goblets from a wine barrel near the end of the table.

"Drink hearty!" I grinned.

Hurriedly, our eyes on the entrance, we ate and drank. The wine was bracing and the pears were delicious. Robogardens and pseudovineyards paid off for Kane and, at the moment, I was glad that he enjoyed the finer things in life.

We kept moving.

More hallways. Corridors. Rooms with medieval furniture, with paintings of dukes and earls and kings. Italian nearmarble floors. Stone fireplaces with stuffed boars' heads mounted above them.

And, finally, the outer portcullis.

To shield my displaced nose I pretended to be blowing it. I kept my head down and we were passed through; the drawbridge was lowered and we crossed over.

"Sam, we *made* it!" exclaimed Esma, as the drawbridge was raised behind us.

"Not quite," I said. "Look what's around the bend."

Kane's fire-breathing dragon was sleeping soundly in the road. His huge scaly body filled the road's entire width; there was a sheer drop on either side and no room to wriggle past.

We were effectively blocked.

"That's one hell of a place to take a snooze," I said.

"He won't like it if we disturb him," Esma said. "What are we going to do?"

I was trying to figure an answer to that question when the castle alarm blared: Waaaaa-eeee-waaaaa! Waaaaa-waaaaa!

"Jig's up!" I said. "They must have found our three stiffs in the Tower." I jerked out my .38 and handed it to Esma. "Take this. You'll be needing it."

The drawbridge was beginning to swing down, which

meant that the castle guards would be streaming across it at our backs while Kane's pet continued to block the road down to the village.

I figured he must have had a hard night because he was still snoozing despite the siren shrill of the alarm.

"Watch the dragon!" I told Esma. "Yell if he wakes up."

I left her there and scrambled up the road to its edge, hauled out the sawed-off flexbarrel .60-20 laserbeam and took a sight on the half-lowered drawbridge.

I pressed the release stud—and a bright beam sliced into the bridge like a knife through warm cheese. Within moments I'd cut the bridge in half. The two pieces tumbled down into the boiling lava.

Which fixed the castle guards. They could no longer reach us.

Now all I had to worry about was the fire-dragon and the rest of the soldiers in the village below us. Even if we could slip by the dragon how could—

"Sam! Sam, he's waking up!" Esma yelled. "You'd better come quick."

I did just that, and by the time I reached Esma the big scaly devil was up on his feet and plenty mad. It was a cinch he didn't like sirens and falling drawbridges and private ops disturbing his afternoon nap. His boulder-big red-flecked eyes glared down at us, and his long spiked tail swung back and forth like an Earthcrane.

"Get back," I warned Esma. "I think he's going to—"

He did.

The huge mouth gaped open like hell's own furnace and a long gout of yellow-white flame lashed out. It seared and blackened the road in front of us.

"I guess he's still a little sleepy," I said. "His aim's off. Missed by a good three feet."

"Oh, Sam, he'll incinerate both of us!"

"No, he won't," I told her. I had the laserbeam and felt

93

confident. If it could slice through a drawbridge it should be able to clobber a dragon.

I aimed at the massive pebbled head and pressed the stud.

Nothing!

I tried again. Still nothing. The gun had jammed on me just when I needed it most.

I tossed the damn thing aside and pulled out the Kid's .20-40 Vickers, a toy next to the laser, but all I had.

Before I could squeeze off a shot another long blast of flame flashed out of the dragon's mouth and I leaped back, stumbling. My left foot struck a rock and twisted under me. I fell, and the Vickers was knocked from my hand. It tumbled over the edge of the road, gone.

The angry dragon reared above me, tall as a rocket, all green and purple scales and glittering pebbled skin and monstrous fire-flecked eyes. Smoke streamed from its cave-wide nostrils.

I was in trouble. In another second I'd be cooked meat; even a groggy dragon couldn't miss three times out of three.

"Sam . . . here!" yelled Esma. She had retreated to the bend in the road, watching the struggle. Now she sprinted toward me, waving the .38.

"Throw it!" I shouted to her. "Toss it to me!"

She did, and I caught it neatly, swinging to face my scaly friend. I took another split-second to aim; if I missed there wouldn't be another chance. I was convinced of that.

I went for the eyes. Two shots, spaced just far enough apart for me to swing the barrel from left eye to right. One wouldn't do it; I had to shatter them both.

A roar of pain. A trumpeting of anger and surprise. The great blind head swiveled fiercely. Flame roared from the angry upturned mouth.

Now I had the advantage. I fired again—two, three,

four times, putting my shots into the head. Until the .38 clicked empty.

The big boy staggered, roaring. His forked tongue danced like a kite. His feet smashed boulders as he stamped out his fury. Smoke was pouring from his eyes and nose.

"You *got* him, Sam!" enthused Esma, helping me stand up. My left ankle was sprained; walking would be murder.

Above us, the giant's body quaked. He staggered, tail lashing fitfully. We ducked as it swished over our heads.

"Back!" I warned. "He's about to go!"

Like a falling granite mountain the green and purple giant crashed down into the road, expiring in a great hiss of steam. The tail lashed in a final, convulsive movement. And was still.

We approached him. A spreading pool of black was darkening the road around the mountainous carcass.

"Blood!" gasped Esma, putting a hand to one of her mouths.

"No," I said. "Oil."

"You mean he was—"

"A robot, what else? Kane's pet robot dragon. I just ruptured his crankcase."

"Amazing!" exclaimed Esma in hushed admiration. "What a truly amazing creation."

"They don't call Kane the Robot King for laughs," I said. "He knows how to put the wheels and cogs together. I'm sure he designed this baby himself."

Esma peered into one of the shattered eye cavities. "Gears," she said. "I see gears in there. And pipes. Long pipes and hoses."

"For the fire and smoke," I said.

"I just can't get over how lifelike he was!"

"Well, you'd better," I said. "We've got company."

I pulled Esma down behind the dragon's smoking

head as a horde of hornet-mad synthetics boiled up the road toward us.

"Can you stop them?"

I sighed. "My ankle's on the fritz. The Kid's gun is gone. My .38's empty. And the laserbeam's jammed. I hate to tell you, sister, but right now the only thing that's gonna save us is a miracle."

Sixteen

We got one. A miracle, that is. At least that's what I thought it was at the time.

One second we were there, crouched behind the leaky robot dragon, with maybe two hundred of Kane's armed guards piling in on us, and the next second we were not there at all.

We were sitting on the floor of Nathan Oliver's lab under the Chicago Art Institute with old Nate dancing a circle around us and clapping his fat pink hands in delight.

"Did it! Did it! Did it! Oh, boy, it worked! It really worked!"

"What worked?" I asked him.

"My timesnapper," Nate told me. "I've been puttering for months trying to get the bugs out of it. Works on the snap-beam principal. You snap-beam things back and forth in time. I snapped a turtle into 3028, give or take a year, but I lost him. The future's pretty foggy. Then I tried to snap up a cop on a horse from Times Square back when cops still rode horses. Well, I got the horse but a 42nd St. wino was riding him. So I gave him a drink and sent him back."

"The horse?" asked Esma.

"No, the wino. I kept the horse."

"Listen, Nate . . ." I stood up; my ankle throbbed but it was easier to walk on. "How the hell did you know where we were and what was happening to us? How did you know we needed to be snap-beamed out of there?"

"That's not easy to explain in layman's terms."

"Try," I said.

"First," he declared, helping Esma to her feet, "I'm going to fix a drink for this charming young creature." He hesitated, jowls quivering. "Or . . . or should I fix you *three* drinks?"

"One's fine," she said. "I usually switch heads with a drink, giving a sip or two to each."

Nate was fascinated. "And you have three different sets of taste buds?"

"Naturally. Just as I have three brains, three necks, three noses and three sets of eyes and ears."

"That's amazing," said Oliver. "With three brains don't your thoughts get all crossed up? I have a terrible time with *one*."

"Hey, Nate," I said, grabbing his elbow. "Cut the gab and fix her drink. And one for me while you're at it. Make it potent."

After Nate delivered the booze we all sat down in his crowded liveroom. He'd made chairs out of old famous actors. I sat down on Marlon Brando and Esma sat down on Johnny Weissmuller and Nate sat down on Zazu Pitts.

I slugged down the double bourbon like baby's milk. Knocking off giant fire dragons builds a man's thirst. "Okay," I said, as one of Esma's heads sipped at her Scotch and water, "fill me in on just *how* you found us."

Nate squirmed uncomfortably. "It's complicated, Sam."

"So's life," I snapped. "Give!"

Nate sighed, puffing his red-Santa cheeks. "Well . . . when did you see me last?"

"I saw *one* of you when I started this case," I told him. "But that Oliver was in another universe. You—or, rather, the other you—managed to foul up in getting me back here and sent me on another dimensional track. I was plenty steamed over it."

"I guess I wasn't doing too well at that stage," he declared sadly. "The other me, I mean."

"You were a little addlepated," I said. "But your intentions were sound."

"Thanks. That's mighty decent of you."

"So as to when I saw *you* last . . . I'd say that was about a year ago when you asked me to check on that missing electronic cow of yours."

"Ah, yes," sighed Nate. "I feared she'd been stolen by another would-be electronic cow-inventor. But it turned out she'd simply wandered away. A loose hoof connection was responsible for her erratic behavior."

"A drunk was half-electrocuted trying to milk her in the middle of Michigan Avenue," I reminded him.

"Yes." A fresh sigh. "My inventions seem to attract inebriates. The wino on the horse, for example."

"Where's all this leading?" I wanted to know.

"To my explanation, of course. I merely wanted to fill you in on what's been happening since last we met."

"Then snap to it."

Nate laced and unlaced his pudgy fingers. There was no way of rushing him, so I built me another double bourbon and settled back into Brando's stomach to hear Nate out. Esma seemed amused—and Oliver's having time-yanked us out of KublaKane had put her in a good mood. Besides, since her father was one, she was used to nutty scientists.

"After the unfortunate Michigan Avenue incident with the startled drunk," Nate said, "I turned away from electronic cows to more exacting forms of creative endeavor. I tentatively entered the area of time and parallel universes, getting my toes wet, one might say, in the great cosmic stream."

"I'd heard you were into that schmazz," I said.

"Indeed I was." He removed a huge Irish linen handkerchief and blew his nose like a trumpet. Then he continued. "My ultimate achievement was the time snap-beam device which I employed in your rescue." He gave us a smirk. "It is a sort of spy hole into past and future. When the charged neutron isoten energy vibrations are in their proper cohesive sonic sequence I have, in effect, a *window* through which I may peer at past and future events. It's no cinch to set up, however."

"And that's what you used to spot us with?" I was on my third bourbon, feeling mellow and relaxed. My ankle had quit aching. Just for the hell of it, I switched chairs and sat down on Veronica Lake. Esma stayed with Weissmuller.

"Yes," Nate answered my question with a fresh smirk. "I was doing a bit of poking about in the near-present and picked up your energy pattern on Mercury."

"Were you in on the whole scene?" I asked. "Did you see me stiff the dragon?"

"Indeed I did. And a fine display of cool nerve and superb marksmanship it was!"

I gave him smirk for smirk. "Nothing to it."

"In fact," Oliver went on, "I became so deeply engrossed in your dramatic battle for survival I almost forgot about time-snapping you to safety."

"You got us out and that's what matters," said Esma. "We're very much in your debt, Mr. Oliver."

Nate flushed with pleasure. "It is always gratifying to a creator when his inventions benefit those who may need assistance."

I waved my glass at him. "Got to find out something, Nate."

He inclined his fat head toward me, waiting.

"Where are we, right now, in relation to where we were in KublaKane?"

Oliver laced his hands again. "As precisely as I can determine, you are about an Earthday in front of yourself."

"Meaning we picked up twenty-four hours?"

"About that. Give or take a squidge."

"Ok," I said, putting my empty glass on a coffee table shaped like Alan Ladd. "That gives us a little leeway on Kane. If we'd ended up a day *behind* ourselves he might have been able to make another attempt on Dr. Umani's life."

"We'd better contact father and tell him we're safe," declared Esma.

"Nope," I said, shaking my head. "Kane might have his vid tapped. We're better off just popping back unannounced. He'll be safe enough till we get there." I shook hands with Nate. "Thanks for the free buggy ride!"

"My pleasure, Sam."

Esma gave him a kiss on the cheek with each pair of lips. He twittered. "Care for another drink?"

"We gotta cut out for Bubble City," I told him.

"But I have more inventions to show you. I'm working on a method in which I may painlessly turn pigs inside out."

"Whatever *for?*" Esma wanted to know.

Nate looked confused. "I'm not sure, to be entirely truthful. There's really no demand for inside-out pigs, is there?"

"Look, we'll take a raincheck on the porkers," I said. "But you could do one more thing for us."

"Simply name it."

"Esma can't hop all the way back to Mars in a guardsman's cape. Got anything else she could wear?"

"I would imagine so," he said, leading us to the bed-booth. He thumbed open a wall, sifted through racked clothing. "How's this?" He showed us a ladies fullsuit, waist-ribbed with slashcut sleeves. "My late wife was quite fond of it."

"I didn't know you'd been married," said Esma.

"Yes. Dorothy worked with me in some of my earlier experiments. She was carried off and strangled by a

101

mechanical ape. I wasn't much good with my apes in those days. They kept going haywire on me."

"How sad!" Esma declared, slipping into the fullsuit. A perfect fit.

Nate got another triplekiss and we beat it.

Seventeen

Before leaving Earth we'd purchased a safe shipment of coldpacs for old Umani—which had allowed Esma to right away slip the doc into a fresh body. He was plenty fed up with being a giraffehead.

When he came out of his labunit to thank me for saving Esma he was a fullblood Oklahoma Cherokee. I explained why my nose was crooked and why I was wearing the face of Kid Smiley, how there hadn't been time for me to get my regular mug restored before picking up the coldpacs.

"Ug! You catchum heap fine bodies," he grunted, using another of his lousy fake accents. "Me likeum this one you betchum!"

"I figure I deserve a reward for bringing back your daughter," I told him.

He nodded his sun-bronzed head. "Great Spirit say you brave man. Me reward you with bonus. Plenty wampum!"

"That's not the kind of reward I mean. You're paying me enough. I'm not after credits."

"Then you tellum chief what want. Me giveum."

"I want you to stop stalling me on your experiment. I want a full rundown on what you've been fiddling around with and I want to know why F. is trying to stop you."

We looked at each other. His clouded Indian eyes were fierce, and I thought he'd refuse. But he didn't.

"Very well then, Mr. Space," he said. "Your request is most certainly valid and you've earned the right to have it granted. Please follow me and I'll explain everything."

He swung toward his lab and I was right behind him. Verlag blocked me at the door. Bald. Ham-fisted. Red-eyed. A huge chunk of fighting meat who looked as if he'd put his life on the line to keep me out of that lab.

"Tell your loyal first cousin here to drop the riot pose," I said to Umani. "Tell him I've been invited to the party."

"Allow Mr. Space to enter. Stand aside, man!"

Verlag stood aside, glaring. I gave him a glare of my own and entered the lab.

All labs look alike to me. This one looked like Nate Oliver's lab, which looked like most others: tubes, vats, bottles, voltage gimmicks, wires, cables, bubbling fluids. One of Esma's heads was lowered over the eyepiece of a gadget on one of the long tables; her other two heads looked up at me as I came in. "Sam! I didn't think Daddy would—"

"Would let me in on the family secrets?" I grinned. "I earned the info and he knows it."

Umani Indian-nodded, hands folded across his chest. He dug playing chief. Too bad the body was dressed in a plain bizsuit; he needed feathers and buckskin and buffalo horns to go with the pose.

Esma was happy for me. "I hated hiding things from you, Sam. But Daddy insisted."

"Ug. That true. Chief tell daughter keep mouths shut."

"Now we'll tell him everything, won't we, Daddy?"

Verlag stepped between us, crazy-eyed. "I say we keep this cheap peeper in the dark about the setup," he rasped. "He could be working for F.—trying to sneak his way into our confidence."

"Verlag, you're a bloody fool!" snapped Umani. "Leave us at once. You've just insulted the man who saved Esma's life."

"I still say it could be a con," snarled Verlag.

"Out! Away!" demanded Umani.

Verlag slunk off, glaring back at me.

"I must apologize for my first cousin, Mr. Space," said Umani. "He's been working night and day. All these lurid attacks on me have put him under something of a strain. In addition to which, as an out-of-temper giraffe-head, I was not the best of lab companions."

"Forget it," I said. "Just tell me what goes with your experiment."

"Ah, but of course." Umani moved to a squared-off area in one corner of the unit. It had been cleared of junk. Just bare flooring. "The balls, my dear," he said to Esma.

She brought him two red rubber balls, one much larger than the other.

"Ug. You watchum balls," grunted Umani. He tossed them onto the bare flooring. The balls bounced once, then rose in the air. The small one began circling the large one, which continued to float free of the floor.

"What the hell goes on?" I asked. "What are a couple of dumb balls supposed to prove?"

Umani gave me an Indian scowl. "White man not give chief chance to tellum. Shutum mouth, watchum balls."

"The balls represent the Earth circling the Sun," Esma told me. "Normally, the Earth orbits smoothly—but it *can* be affected."

Umani threw a toggle switch and the smaller ball began to weave drunkenly. It finally lost contact and fell to the floor.

"I still don't get it," I said.

Umani drew his heavy Cherokee brows together in a deep frown. "The Earth is is trouble. It is no longer stable. Its natural orbit around the sun has already shifted. To the average solar citizen the shift is not yet perceptible. The same situation is true of Mars. All of the planets within the System are being subtly manipulated."

"What are you telling me?"

"Isn't it obvious? Someone is affecting the orbital patterns of all the solar bodies in our System. The change is not yet critical, but the danger is very real. If something is not done to counteract these orbital shifts . . ."

"Our goose is cooked. And you've been trying to uncook it, right?"

"Exactly. My experiment, which I have dubbed ORSTA, orbit stabilizer, is designed to re-establish the correct orbital patterns. But I'm working against terrible odds. I'm not sure I can finish in time to save the System."

I perched on a closewood workstool and tried to absorb the info. "What I don't get is why. Why would anyone try to freak up the System? If the nine planets and their satellites all go kablooey wouldn't whoever's behind it go with them?"

Umani sighed. "I think not. Whoever is causing this orbital shift obviously has a base *outside* our System and will no doubt conduct the final phase of destruction from there. Just think of it: nine planets driven into collision orbit with one another. A cosmic game of mibs, played by an evil child."

"To what purpose?"

Umani shrugged. "I cannot guess. Ways of white man strange to Indian. Great Spirit angry. Chief confused."

"Are you the only scientist working on this?"

"Heavens, no. I've been in contact with dozens of others throughout the System. But, as it seems, I am the only one who is close to solving the problem. That's why my life has been in constant jeopardy."

I slapped my hands together. "Wow. This is *some* can of beans! The whole System. Kablooey! Whoever's behind it doesn't do things in a small way."

"Father thinks Kane may be the one," put in Esma. "And since he engineered my kidnap the idea is reasonable."

I argued the point. "Kane has a lot of personal business interests in the System. Why would he destroy his own solar empire?"

"A good question," agreed Umani. "And one to ponder."

"How long will it take for you to get your orbit stabilizer cooking?"

"Perhaps a week or so, Marstime, if I am allowed to work sans attack. By then I should be able to steady the orbital shift and save the System."

"Well, my job's over. I'm going to head for Callisto and get my face back."

Esma looked worried. "Aren't you going after Kane?"

"What for?"

"To find out if he's really F. And because he tried to murder all of us. And because he had me kidnapped. And because—"

I stopped her. "Whoa! Everything you say is true, but what can I do about it? We have no solid proof against Kane, legally speaking. I'm just one guy. I can't face Kane alone."

"But you went after him twice before," Esma protested. "In Domeville and at Whisker Town. Why then and not now?"

"My curiosity was roused. I didn't know who F. was then. Now it appears he's Ronfoster Kane and if that's so then he's out of reach. Too big a fish for me to net. Can't you see that?"

Esma nodded all three heads. "Forgive me, Sam. I just wasn't thinking straight. I was letting emotion overcome logic. There's no sense in your facing down Kane. We hired you for a job and the job's done. You have every right to quit."

"I'm not quitting if you still want me around. I could stay here with your father until his gimmick is working."

"No, Daddy's safe enough here in the lab. The unit is now destructproof, and we have Verlag on hand."

"Swell," I said. "You can reach me on Mars if you need me for anything."

"Thank you, Sam." She leaned toward me and kissed my cheek with her nearest head.

"Hey," I said. "I forgot about Nicole. Where *is* she?"

"Daddy said she left shortly after you did. Told him she had to return to Allnew York."

"That right. Daughter speak truth."

"Did she say why?"

"Not say why. Just leave. Take great bird in sky and go far place."

I rubbed a slow hand over my neck. "I thought we had something going. Thought she'd wait for me. Did she leave any message?"

Umani shook his bronzed head.

"So be it," I shrugged. "Guess I must be losing my touch with dames."

Two of Esma's three heads blushed. "I wouldn't exactly say that, Sam."

Which restored my masculine ego and sent me chuckling on my way.

Eighteen

On Callisto Zaadar seemed a little miffed about my bending Kid Smiley's nose—as if I'd spoiled a picture he'd painted—but he put me back in jimdandy shape. I got my ugly old kisser back, good as new.

I was glad to be myself again.

In Bubble City I had a surprise waiting for me: Nicole was sitting in my office when I arrived.

"Thought you'd cut for Allnew York," I said.

"I did. But I came back to Mars for a very important reason."

She was wearing a deepdelish spackgown with beamed thrusters, and I couldn't resist her. I slid around the desk and took her by the shoulders. Tipped her head back. Kissed her. She had moonfruit lipice on her earlobes and I found that erotic as hell. "Just couldn't stay away, baby. Isn't that it?"

"No, Sam. That isn't it."

"Huh? I don't get you."

"Maybe this will help explain why I'm here." She pointed a .40-80 twintrack Browning-Pritchett angle-thrust trigweapon at my lower gut.

"Hey! What's wrong with you?"

"Not a thing, Sam. But if you don't do as I say there'll be plenty wrong with *you*. First, put your .38 on the desktop."

Her eyes told me she wasn't kidding.

I followed orders.

109

"Now come with me. I have a ship outside." She gave me a grim little smile. "Back in Allnew York you escorted me. Now it's my turn to escort you."

"Where to?"

"To a man who's waiting to see you."

"And who would that be?"

The smile widened in a wicked flash of teeth. "Ronfoster Kane. Who else?"

"You're some sweet cookie," I told her. "First you play decoy for a sap job—and I end up in another universe. Next you let Kane's gungoons know I was heading for Jupiter and as a result I get brainwashed by mice and shipped off to hunt Zubu eggs. Now you pop up again all set to kidnap me for Mr. Kane. There's just one thing I'd like to know."

"That phrase is pointless and cliched. We all want to know *much* more than just one thing, but people keep saying otherwise. Particularly private detectives. But I'll oblige. What one thing do you wish to know, Sam?"

"Why did you bother to unscramble me on Pluto? Why didn't you just leave me there? Why the Act of Mercy?"

"We've no time to discuss behavioral patterns and character motivation," she said crisply. "The ship is waiting."

"And what if I don't go?"

"You'll go."

I went.

And woke up on Uranus with another terrible headache.

The reason I knew I was on Uranus was that Ronfoster Kane told me I was. They'd put me in a holdchair and the Robot King was standing in front of me, smiling, enjoying the situation. Kane was very tall, at least seven feet, and his eyes were totally black, without visible pupils. His teeth were made from various precious stones—

rubies in front, diamond molars for heavy chewing and emerald incisors. He wore a hammered-silver roomsuit with matching gold-leaf gloves on his steel fingers.

"You are in my quarters on Uranus, Mr. Space," he said. "Nicole was forced to stun you with a head charge. But no harm has been done to you—yet."

I squirmed against the holdchair. "This thing is pinching me," I said.

"Release!" Kane told the chair.

I stood up, stretched my legs, and looked the joint over. We were in what appeared to be a workden. Desk. Faxbooks. Pseudofireplace. Dark nearbeam ceiling. Comfy.

"Why did you have me brought here?"

Kane's teeth glittered and flashed under the denlights. "My curiosity impelled me," he said. "How, I asked myself, could one sleazy third-rate private op walk into KublaKane and remove my prisoner, Esma Umani, kill my superbly-engineered fire dragon, cut my drawbridge in half and then vanish like marsh mist with the girl before the eyes of two hundred and six trained guardsmen? I asked myself that thorny question. Now, having gone to the trouble of fetching you here, I put the same question to you."

"How did we vanish like marsh mist?"

"How indeed?"

I figured some true scam wouldn't hurt anybody. "We were time-snapped out of there by an old pal of mine who has invented a device that snaps people back and forth in time."

"And you expect me to believe that?"

I nodded.

Kane puckered his lower lip, thinking. Then he unpuckered. "All right, I believe it."

"Then am I free to leave?"

"Certainly not." Kane's all-black eyes glowed. "I naturally intend to dispose of you. You are annoying. In fact, you have done nothing but annoy me from the moment Dr. Umani hired you. I kill people who annoy me. Simple logic."

"Look, Kane, how come you're trying to jiggle nine planets out of orbit? What's your game?"

Kane frowned darkly. "Again, you annoy me. Instead of asking me questions I expected you to attack me. We are alone here and I just told you I intended to destroy you and since you are trained in sixteen forms of solar combat—"

"Seventeen," I corrected.

"—in seventeen forms of solar combat I naturally assumed you would attack me. I was really looking forward to it."

"Sorry to disappoint you but I'm not doing anything in the way of attacking right now. Going for your throat would be a dopey move."

"But why?" Kane spread his gloved hands. "I'm alone. I have no weapon. I'm totally vulnerable to attack."

I shook my head. "You're not really alone because this is one of your prime hangouts. The joint is no doubt crawling with roboguards. Secondly, you are not weaponless. I happen to know you have steel arms and legs which are pretty deadly and could mess me up a lot. Okay?"

Kane pouted for a moment, then aimed a jeweled smile at me. "You're absolutely correct, of course. If you attacked me I'd cheerfully inflict serious damage on your person, rendering you incapable of fighting for your life in the arena I have selected for your death. You'll need all your strength for that."

Kane brought one of his steel arms down savagely on the holdchair in which I'd previously been sitting. The chair was smashed and split by the blow.

"See what your innate wisdom has done for you, Mr. Space. Your bones would have snapped like the breadsticks of Earth."

I gave him my wise-owl grin.

"You are something of an expert on machinery, are you not?"

"I wouldn't say that. I know guns, and I can take a jet-cab apart."

"You'll appreciate this," said Kane, and slipped out of his hammered-silver roomsuit. He stood naked in front of me. "It is not often that I have the opportunity to display my superb arms and legs to a man who appreciates machinery."

His torso was flesh. The rest was metal. He even had iron balls, which surprised me, and I said so.·

"Ah, yes," Kane smiled. "I had this set of custom genitals made up from my own designprints."

"But why iron balls?"

"They are detachable. Very effective in close battle. I have killed several enemies with my detachable balls."

"I can see the advantage," I admitted. I tapped his right arm. "Does it come off too?"

"Of course. Would you like to examine it?"

"Love to," I said.

Kane unscrewed his right arm with his left. "A bit clumsy."

"Take your time," I told him.

He passed his arm to me. "Here you are."

I turned it slowly in my hands, marveling aloud at the smooth elbow and wrist jointing. Then I hit Kane on the head with it.

Hard.

He looked surprised and personally betrayed. "I—I'm quite disappointed in you, Mr. Space," he muttered groggily.

Then he fell flat on his face.

Nineteen

I locked the workden door from the inside, mixed myself a double bourbon, and sat down in Kane's comfy-couch to think things over.

The Robot King didn't stir. He was out cold and wouldn't be waking up for awhile—so I was in no big rush. For one reason: I had nowhere to go.

In the hallway, I knew, Kane's guards were posted. With more guards on the grounds. And yet more at the launchport. Even if I could find a weapon here in the workden and even if I managed to shoot my way out of the house I'd never be able to leave Uranus alive.

I decided to see what I could find in Kane's desk. I finished my drink, walked over and gave the desk a professional sift.

Which got me nowhere. If Kane had any plans for throwing the System out of whack they sure weren't in his desk.

Then I got the bright idea of searching Kane. And came away with his hypno-ring. It was on the index finger of the unscrewed arm I'd put him to sleep with. I'd heard about Kane's ring; it used a rapid lightbeam spin-effect to induce an instant hypnotic trance in any subject, human or alien. I told myself it was too bad the ring didn't work on synthetics. Kane's guards were impervious to hypnotism, so I couldn't use the ring to escape.

I gave the walls a going-over and, sure enough, a case

114

of faxbooks near the pseudofireplace slid back revealing what could only be a secret passage. A way out? I'd soon know.

The passageway wasn't quite high enough for me, so I moved forward in a half-crouch. I didn't know what kind of problems I'd run into but anything was better than being stuck back in the workden with Kane. He wouldn't be too friendly toward me when he woke up. The farther away from him I could get the better off I'd be.

The passage snaked right, then left. At least there were no side tunnels to confuse things—and I could see where I was running: the tunnel was brightly illumined and lined, top and sides, in a white, cork-like substance that kept out dampness. It was one of the neatest secret passages I'd ever run through. No spiders or bats or cobwebs here.

It began to get narrower. Looked as if I was going to get some answers pronto. Ahead, a black door. Smooth. No handle or knob. I couldn't pull on it—so I pushed. Harder. The door gave, and I stepped into . . .

. . . into a *candy forest!*

The trees were striped peppermint with green sugar-leaves. The path under my feet was made of licorice, and the stream that chuckled and bubbled beside the road was—I tasted it—orange soda pop. There were giant jellybean boulders in the stream and chocolate bushes were growing everywhere along the banks.

I stood on the gumdrop grass above the soda pop stream trying to dope things. A slight creaking behind me. The door was swinging shut! I made a dive for it and grabbed the edge, yet it kept closing. I pulled away my fingers to keep them from getting mashed as the black door clonked shut.

Leaving me in the candy forest.

Okay, roads lead somewhere. This one, I hoped, was no exception. I'd run it out and see where it took me.

Deeper into the heart of the forest. No other sounds.

Just my feet slap-slapping down the licorice path. I was getting a bit winded but I kept at a fast trot; I wanted to clear the forest and reach some natural terrain. Kane's sugar-spun landscape didn't appeal to me. It was just another example of his twisted sense of humor. A candy forest on Uranus I could damn well do without.

But it was beginning to get to me. All the candy. Tons of candy. I was suddenly starved for something sweet. I grabbed a handful of chocolate roses, chewing as I ran. They were delicious. Yummy.

Gripped by sudden, intense thirst I stopped to belly down beside the stream and lap up some orange soda pop. It was even sweeter than the chocolate roses! Wow.

I took a large bite out of a peppermint tree trunk, gobbled up fistfuls of gumdrop grass, finally knelt down and bit into the road. I've always had a yen for licorice and this stuff was great.

I was sitting, cross-legged in the road like a big kid, sucking on a candycane tree-root when the witch landed in front of me.

No doubt about what she was. Big black peaked hat. Broomstick. Long tacky gray dress full of rips and patches. Hooked nose, with a fat hairy wart at the end. Blood-red lips. Yellow snag teeth. Squinty eyes. Dirty hair poking out from the hat.

She was snarling. "How *dare* you come along here and begin eating up my forest!" She stomped a gnarled foot.

"It's not your forest," I said. "It's Kane's forest. And he owes me a few goodies. I'm a kidnap victim and the least he can do is feed me."

She was hopping mad. I know, because she began hopping around me in the road, shaking her broom in the air, and doing a lot of shrieking. "My dark curse on ye! May the demons of fire toast your skin! May the demons of the wind scour the hair from your head! May the demons of the sea send waves black and terrible to drown you!"

116

"Thanks for the good wishes," I said. "Now, buzz off, sister. I've got to get trotting."

As real as she looked she was obviously one of Kane's robots, like the dragon, and if she tried anything fancy I'd be happy to separate her cogs. She jumped back as I stood up.

"Scat!" I growled.

She shook the broom at me, cackling, and little sparks danced out the end of it and settled over me in a sparkly shower.

"Rigga ree, Rigga dee!
Curse descend now upon thee!
Rigga do, Rigga day!
Let fire and wind and water slay!"

She had a good act. But I was bored with it. I gave her a shove and she fell backwards into the soda pop stream. The second her body touched the surface she began to hiss and bubble and dissolve. She didn't last long. Her pointy hat was the only thing left on the surface as the bubbles settled.

I moved on down the road.

Would any more of Kane's kooky creations show up to bug me? Maybe I'd meet a gingerbread man. Or a tin woodsman. Or a sugar plum fairy. If so, I could handle them.

Maybe I'd even run into a soda pop mermaid.

I was slowing. My legs ached and my lungs were giving out. Enough is enough. When would this dumb forest end? How big *was* it anyhow?

The sun was getting mighty hot. I didn't know if it was a real sun or a phony one Kane had put up there but heat is heat and I was beginning to sweat like a Tarmanian sand-wrestler.

Ha! I grinned to myself: there's the first curse, eh? The curse of the fire demons.

I quit grinning when my clothes began to smoke. They were actually burning! I tried to beat out the flames but

117

couldn't make any headway. I didn't wait; I plunged into the soda pop stream.

It put out the fire okay, with no pain. But my clothes were singed off. I was buck naked.

And a wind was rising.

The peppermint trees began to sway; the sky darkened; the bushes bent and swished around my feet. I leaned into the wind and pushed forward.

The damn road couldn't go on forever.

I felt the wind tugging at my hair and remembered the witch-curse. The ugly old crone had been telling it straight because I felt my scalp loosen and whip away behind me.

I was as bald as an egg.

A roaring. Not the wind. Another kind of roar. Growing louder. I froze, tried to figure out what could make a sound like that. Then I knew.

Water. Tons and tons of rushing water. That's what was roaring, advancing, cutting its way through Kane's candy forest.

It hit me. A gigantic green savage wave of it thundered out of the trees, rolling giant jellybean boulders ahead of it, slamming over me with immense force.

I fought to keep my head above water, fought to keep breathing. But it was hopeless. The hungry tide swallowed me in a dark rush of foam.

I spun in an endless ballet deep in the slimed green belly of the wave. Choking water entered my open gasping mouth. My lungs filled, and burst . . .

Twenty

"Mr. Space?"

"Yes."

"Do you know who I am?"

"Yes."

"Tell me who I am."

"You're Ronfoster Kane, the Robot King."

"Excellent. You're completely out of it now."

"Out of what?"

"The trance. You are free of the trance."

"You hypnotized me?" I stared at Kane. Both his arms were firmly attached to his body.

"That is correct, Mr. Space." He chuckled. "You are wondering about my arm, aren't you?"

"Maybe," I said.

"And you're wondering why my head bears no mark from the blow you gave me?"

"Maybe."

"This is because there *was* no blow. You did not, in fact, strike me."

"Hell, I clobbered you! You unscrewed your arm and I used it to—"

"No, you did not," Kane said. He was seated on his comfycouch, legs crossed, enjoying the game. His black eyes gleamed. "The entire action existed only in your mind. I used my ring to induce an instant hypnotic condition and fed the incidents directly into your brain while you were in a trance state."

119

"But—the forest . . . the old witch . . . the water . . ."

"All part of the fun I was having with you," declared Kane. "I allowed you to believe that you had been able to strike me down and escape. Once your mind had accepted this simple fantasy I invented all the rest of it. Or rather, *you* invented it at my suggestion."

I walked over to the wall, ran my hand along it.

"Looking for something?"

"There's a secret tunnel in there," I said.

Kane chuckled. "Solid merdstone I'm afraid. I don't favor secret tunnels, Mr. Space. Too dank and lightless."

"This one was bright and clean."

"Of course. Your mind provided the ideal secret tunnel for you. That which is imagined invariably surpasses that which is real."

"Why?" I asked. "Why the trance trick?"

"It was my way of amusing myself. Quite harmless, really. What happens to you next will not be so harmless. It is time I wipe you from my schedule. My business interests are many and your death is simply a minor item on a rather crowded agenda."

"Does one of the items on that agenda have anything to do with knocking our System cockeyed?"

"No more questions, no more answers," snapped Kane, rising. "Our personal byplay is concluded. On to business."

He moved to a faxcase and pressed a section. The wall in front of the comfycouch folded back to reveal a floor-to-ceiling viewpane, through which I could see a smooth, level area as large as a football field on Earth.

"That is your arena of death," said Kane. "I'll be able to watch you die while seated here on my comfycouch sipping a heated Venusian Rum Delight which my android chef, Pierre, is now preparing for the occasion."

I glared at him, at his damned jeweled smile. "And what will I face out there—another of your pet fire dragons?"

120

"You will discover soon enough who or *what* will kill you. Actually, it would be a pity to spoil the surprise." He nodded toward the dendoor. "You are free to leave."

"And what if I choose to stay right here?"

"Questions, always questions." Kane raised a metal finger. The door popped open and two burly synthetics grabbed me and hauled me away.

When they let me go I was on the field, with Kane's special viewpane to my left. It was opaque on the side facing me and I couldn't see him. But he saw me; his amplified voice boomed over the field.

"You shall need weapons in order to extend the spectacle, Mr. Space. A brave man should die fighting."

I waited, puzzled but alert. A black synthetic appeared, carrying an armload of guns. He dumped them at my feet and left the field.

I checked the booty. Kane had been generous. Here was a .40-903 Noggle-Henry cutbeam screwjoint slicer, a .120-10 boxbleed Heebish-Hoskins boregun and a .43-17½ Kamish-Bibler doublestock jetflare—which was a mean piece of equipment.

All in all, quite a lot of firepower. Was Kane going to give me a real chance to shoot my way out? With weapons such as these I could handle anything.

Kane's voice cracked over the field: "Pick up the first weapon of your choice, Mr. Space, and stand ready. You are about to be attacked."

At least he warned me. I snatched up the Noggle-Henry cutbeam, expecting one of Kane's fantastic creations to appear. Maybe a giant synthogater, or a massive nearelephant. But, once again, Kane surprised me.

The field on which I stood was encircled by a 20-foot wall of featureless rock. A sudden opening in the base of the rock disgorged a dozen Kane synthetics, all bearing normal handweapons. They crossed the field, bearing down on me.

121

"Here they come, Mr. Space," boomed Kane. "Better start shooting."

I did. And it was absurdly easy to cut them down with the Noggle-Henry.

A second wave followed, and I dispatched them just as easily, using the Heebish-Hoskins.

"Your aim is excellent, Mr. Space," Kane told me. "The weapons are self-charging and will remain operative. You should be able to deal with any number of my clumsy, poorly-armed synthetics."

He was right. I could go on knocking over his synthos indefinitely. So what was Kane's game?

The lop-sided battle continued—with me slicing up Kane's robot army, wave after wave. A few synthos managed to fire their handguns at me but the range was too far and I wasn't touched. My hardware had the edge on range.

I still couldn't dope Kane's action.

Then I noticed something; I was slowing down. My aim was not as accurate, even with the boxbleed Heebish-Hoskins. I was tiring fast. But why? This was easy target work, nothing more.

My hands had turned brown. Liver spots had begun to cover them. My eyesight was way off and my legs were shaking.

I was now missing as often as I scored.

"Better try the jetflare, Mr. Space," Kane suggested, and I could hear him chuckle.

I picked up the .43-17½ Kamish-Bibler and did a little better with it, knocking down a whole row of charging synthos with a single jetcharge. But by the next wave my hands were trembling. The Kamish-Bibler was too heavy. I could no longer hold it. The weapon slipped from my fingers.

This wasn't exhaustion; it was something far worse. I looked at the hairs along my wrists. White. My skin was dry and puckered, my cheeks sucked in, my eyes watery and filmed.

I touched my face, ran my fingers over my lips, nose, forehead. My face was withered and dust-dry under my fingers. Now I knew the real enemy Kane was using against me. And how could I fight it; how could I fight old age?

"Be quick, Mr. Space," Kane's voice warned. "More of my synthetics are moving toward you. Soon they'll be within handweapon range. Better get busy, old timer!"

I coughed, a racking bone-shaking cough, and dropped to my knobby knees, scrabbling feebly for the jetflare. I clutched it, raised it to fire, tried to focus on the advancing line of black synthos. Waves of hot dizziness swept across my brain. The field danced and shimmered crazily in front of me.

I turned my wrinkled face toward the dark viewwall, behind which I knew Kane was laughing at me. I shook a withered fist at him as the synthetics moved in.

Trembling, I swung to face their charge.

But they'd stopped. All of them. I peered at dozens of frozen black-marble robots on the wide field. Kane had deactivated his troops.

And I knew why.

He didn't need them any longer. I was growing older by the moment. I could feel my skin loosen and shrivel; my bones ached; my fingernails cracked and blackened.

Kane was watching an old man die.

Twenty-One

"You'll be gone very soon now, Mr. Space," Kane's confident voice informed me over the fieldspeaker. "Already you are past eighty and aging at the rate of a year a minute. In ten more Earthminutes you'll be over ninety. Your laboring heart will cease beating within its wrinkled sack of bones and desiccated flesh. Your breath will rattle into silence. A final twitch or two—and that will be the end of private operative Samuel T. Space."

He kept gabbing at me as I sat on the field of battle, gasping, shaking, growing weaker by the second.

"In case you are speculating on the possibility of this situation being part of a hypnotrance let me assure you that this is all quite real. You are, in actuality, a wheezing old codger."

The weapons at my feet were useless now. My clothing hung slack on my bony scarecrow's frame; my muscles were loose and flabby, my cheekbones sunken, my lips puckered and seamed. And breathing was a labor, a supreme task that drained my sagging body of its last energy. Kane was right: I wouldn't last for more than another ten minutes or so.

It was a hell of a way for a tough private op to cash in his chips. If Kane stood right in front of me and my .38 was in my hand I couldn't pull the trigger.

I figured I'd just passed a hundred when Nicole popped into three-dimensional reality at my left elbow.

"Hang on, Sam," she yelped, jamming a metal hat on

my white-haired freckled old skull. "We'll be out of this in a jiffy!"

"Shoot them! Fire! Fire!" Kane was yelling—and I saw that he'd reactivated his army of synthos.

They were raising their guns for the kill when Nicole and I popped into another dimension.

We were back in my office on Mars. Nicole was sitting in my client's chair and I was behind my desk. Everything looked normal, except for our metal hats.

"By crackey!" I wheezed, slapping my shriveled old thigh. "That was a mighty fancy rescue. How'd you manage it?"

"Simple," said Nicole. "I vamped a key to the storage unit out of one of Kane's men and borrowed two Portahat transporters. The same type, basically, that those goons used on you back in Allnew York."

"But how come we're still wearing them?" I croaked, fingering my warm metal hat. "Aren't they supposed to snap back into their own universe?"

"Not *these* kind," she replied. "They're equipped for multiple entry, universe to universe. The model they used on you was the pop-back one, designed to leave a person stranded in another world. That was the Portahop J-9zzzz. I made sure I got the J-9xxxx ones—the non-hoppers."

"Hah! Awk! Foof!" I coughed and hacked and sneezed, as incredibly-old men are inclined to do.

"You should learn to swallow your sneezes," Nicole told me. "I practiced until I could. I'm an expert on the Theory of Sneezes."

"Humbug!" I rasped, wiping my lumpy nose. "Where the deuce are we? And why save me after kidnapping me?"

"We're in the closest universe I could dial," she said. "And I saved you because I'm in love with you."

"But look at the differences in our ages," I said. "You're

125

twenty-something and I'm over a hundred. These May-December things never work out."

She giggled. "You've still got your sense of humor, Sam. And that's good to know. Proves you're not yet senile."

"I'm damn close to being," I said grumpily. "But you still haven't explained why you kidnapped me."

"I was under Kane's power," she said, wrinkling her freckled nose. "He used his hypno ring on me to induce a trance. Then he instructed me to go to Mars and bring you to him. I just wasn't myself, Sam."

I gave her an old man's snarl. "You're always trapping me and then saving me."

"That's true," she sighed. "I seem to continually fall into evil clutches. Then I'm corrupted, blackmailed, tortured and hypnotized. It's very discouraging. Guess I'm what they call a natural victim. But right now I love you and that's what matters. Love is cleansing and all-powerful."

She kissed my sunken left cheek. "Ouch. Your white spiny old whiskers scratch."

I spread my liver-spotted hands on the desk. "How in dang-tootin' am I gonna regain my lost years? People just won't hire hundred-year-old private eyes. Tarnation! I can barely totter."

"Don't worry," Nicole said softly, patting my bald dome, "Something or someone will turn up."

Someone did. Me. Not I. Me. The one who owned this office in this universe. He walked in and there I was.

"Hello, Nicole," Sam said. "Who's the old gink, and why is he propped behind my desk wearing that silly metal hat?"

"I'm not your Nicole," she said. "I'm not, in other words, the Nicole you know in your world. I'm an *extra* Nicole from another dimension—and these hats are portable transporters. The man—or rather the old gink—behind your desk, Mr. Space, is actually another you."

"Nuts. I don't look like that," said Sam.

"Of course not. But if you were subjected to an advanced aging process, as he was, by the Robot King you would indeed look exactly that way."

"You mean Kane turned him into this old geezer?"

"*Our* Kane did, not yours. Yours might try it on you or he might not. But that really doesn't concern any of us at the present moment. That's not why we're here."

"Then why *are* you here?"

"To hire you," said Nicole.

I creaked and sputtered in my chair. "Dad drat it, you didn't tell me you were hiring me!"

She smiled. "We need a you in younger form. A stronger you. And now we have him."

Sam walked over to me and peered across the desk at my wizened features. "By God, I think this wrinkled old bag of sticks really *is* me!"

I coughed in his face.

Sam jumped away. "Take it easy, Pops!"

"Then just quit *peering* at me," I said testily.

"Okay, what's the story?" Sam growled. "I need to know where the dice are."

She took a roll of credits from her purse and handed them to him. "We are hiring you to put on a portahat and return to our universe. You'll pop up inside Kane's house on Uranus. I can set the hat for that."

"So what do I do when I get there?"

"You simply creep out of the storage unit to his special killquarters and steal his old-age machine. He keeps all that sort of junk in his killquarters. Anything he uses to kill people with will be in there."

"How will I know my way around the joint?"

"I'll give you a floor plan. The rest will be up to you. Actually, your job should be fairly easy. I've seen the machine and it's not too heavy. You shouldn't have any difficulty bringing it back here to us."

She took off her portahat and showed Sam how to

work the dial. Then she gave him a floor plan of Kane's place, shook his hand and he put on the hat.

"Are you comfortable?"

"Just say when."

"When," said Nicole.

Zap! He was gone.

"We did it!" smiled Nicole. She turned to me with a radiant, impossibly-sweet smile. "Bet he'll be back in no time at all. Now, aren't you glad we hired you?"

I didn't reply. In fact, I barely heard her. My ancient old frame was all tuckered out. My eyes slid closed. I sighed, snuffled—and drifted into sleep.

Twenty-Two

"Wake up, Pops!"

It was Sam. He was shaking me.

"Dad drat it!" I pulled myself up, hacking and coughing. I blinked at Sam, my eyes watering.

"Hard to believe this ole jelly bag is really me," he said to Nicole.

"He's you," she nodded. "If you ever manage to live past a hundred in this world you'll look exactly like he does now."

"Then I hope some gungoon puts me on ice first," Sam declared. "Phew!"

I vigorously blew my nose, wiped my rhummy eyes, and asked, "Well—did you get it?"

"You mean did I get the age machine?" Sam looked smug. "Yeah, I got it."

"He was very brave," said Nicole.

"I also got me a shiner," said Sam, probing at his left eye with exploring fingers. The area was purple and puffy. "But I sure messed up them tin guys of Kane's. One of the guards spotted me with the machine just outside Kane's killquarters and seven of 'em jumped me. Gave me a real workout. We rolled around the floor and I thought I was a goner until I got my .38 working. I scattered their tin guts with the ole .38 and that wound up the party."

"He talks even tougher than I do," I said.

"You can see now why we had to send your younger

129

self to steal the machine," Nicole said to me. "At your advanced age you might have suffered a stroke fighting seven big synthetics. All Sam got was a black eye."

"Where's the damn machine?" I wanted to know. "I'm sick of being an old geezer."

"We put it behind your desk near your chair," Nicole said.

"Near *my* chair," snapped Sam.

I tottered from the couch to the desk, with Nicole holding both my elbows to keep me from toppling. I was dizzy after my nap and only half-awake. "What if I die of an attack of gout before we get this thing working?"

"Nonsense," said Nicole. "Gout doesn't strike people down like lightning."

"Old guys always worry," declared Sam. "They're all kinda batty on the subject of health."

"You would be too at over a hundred," I growled. "So shut your ugly yap!"

Sam grinned. "The old timer's still got some fire in his furnace."

"Here we are," said Nicole, guiding me into the chair. I slumped down wearily.

The age machine was round and black and shiny, about the size of a spinkas ball. It had a dial in the front, and a sweepbeam jutted out of the top.

"Hope this dang thing doesn't bring on a toxic condition," I mumbled. "If I get too nervous warts could pop out all over me. I heard what happened once to a nervous oldster."

"Quit fretting and let me adjust the sweep area," said Nicole. "What age do you want to be, Sam?"

"Dunno. Hell, I could be twenty again, couldn't I?" I clapped my withered palms together.

Nicole shook her head. "I wouldn't advise making yourself any younger than you were when the machine aged you. That kind of tinkering could produce negative results."

"She's right, Pops," Sam put in.

I thought it over, nodding my bald skull, and fingering my ropy neck. "Guess there's no use asking for trouble. Set it for thirty-six. That's what I was when Kane began on me."

I realized, at that moment, that Kane must have put me under the machine's influence during the time I thought I was tripping through his candy forest. Which would explain why I hadn't set eyes on the machine before this.

Sam had taken out the office Scotch and offered me the bottle. "How about a jolt for the road?"

"Nope. It could set my ancient heart to racing," I said. "I'll hold off on the booze till I'm thirty-six again."

"Here we go," said Nicole, activating the machine.

The black shiny ball pulsed and shimmered. I felt the beam on me, like a miniature sun, restoring my lost years. My skin tightened; the wrinkles and flab began to disappear; my hair darkened; my cheeks filled out and my gnarled hands became flexible; the liver spots and freckles and heavy blue veins dimmed out, vanishing.

"You're getting younger by the second!" exclaimed Nicole. She turned to share her smile with Sam. And suddenly quit smiling. She gasped.

It was Sam. He was lolling on the floor beside the desk. His pink chubby little face was toothless, his tiny hands lost in the folds of his oversize suit.

"Stop the machine!" I yelled.

Nicole hastily shut it down. The beam flickered out.

We'd goofed. Sam had been caught inside the beam's central sweep area when Nicole had activated the machine. If we hadn't noticed what was happening to him he'd have been reduced to a grease spot by the time I'd reached thirty-six.

"Daaa! Ga, da! Daaada!"

"I think he's trying to say 'Daddy'," Nicole giggled.

131

"This isn't funny," I told her. "We almost killed him. Another few seconds and . . ."

"He's just *darling*," said Nicole, picking little Sam up in her arms and cuddling him. She cooed, clucked at him, pinched his pink cheeks, patted his fat little tummy. "My pwecious wittle pwivate eye," she said in baby-talk. "Him's all wet!"

"Look," I said, snatching Sam away. "This is no time to play Mama. We'll put him back on the floor and reverse the damn machine and get him back to normal."

"But we haven't finished with you," she protested. "You're not nearly young enough yet."

"How old am I?"

"Seventy-one."

I was no kid. But first things first. "Put him under the beam," I told her.

Nicole shrugged. "All right, I'll reverse it and pump him back up to thirty-six. That's the right age for him, isn't it?"

"Guess so," I said. "You dumped us into the nearest parallel universe, didn't you?"

She said she had.

"Okay, then, we're the same age."

"And you have the same enemies!" a harsh frog-toned voice rasped from the doorway. Fruit, Spider and Kid Smiley had walked into the office, all holding guns in their mitts.

"We'll take the machine, Space," snapped Fruit.

"*And* the kid," said Spider. "Just to keep you two from tryin' to nab back the machine." He scooped up little Sammy.

"*And* these portable hats," growled Kid Smiley. "We don't want you jokers jumping into another world for help."

"But why take the machine?" Nicole asked.

Fruit answered with a sneer. "Are you kiddin', lady? We been watchin' that thing work an' it's worth a fortune. Kane don't have nothin' like it in this universe. We figure to sell it to him."

"Yeah," grinned Spider, "for enough jack to retire on."

"Maybe we'll never have to do no more jobs for nobody," said Kid Smiley.

"I wiped all three of you punks out back where I came from," I said. "I can do it again."

"Try anything fancy and little Sammy here buys the big sleep," snapped the Kid.

Fruit bit into a Martian sandpear and the juice ran down his stubbled chin. "You wouldn't want to be responsible for the brat's death, would you, Space? If little Sammy here croaks it'll mean you killed yourself."

"Daaa, da! Gaa, goo!" Sammy said, reaching toward the half-eaten pear.

"We'll let the kid go just as soon as we've sold the machine to Kane," said Spider. He raised a hairy right hand. "An' that's a solemn promise!"

"Yeah," said Fruit. "Just sit tight till we let you know where to pick him up."

"Hah!" I snorted.

"We'll have to trust them, Sam," said Nicole. She looked worried and I didn't blame her any.

Spider picked up the round black age machine. Fruit had Sammy. Kid Smiley kept us covered as they backed slowly out of the office.

The outer door slammed.

They were gone—with six-month-old Sam Space.

And I was seventy-one. Which was still a little too old to go goon hunting.

"What a dumb mess," I groaned, taking out the office Scotch.

At least *it* was properly aged.

Twenty-Three

I was on my third drink, deep in gloom, when I got a brainflash. "Hey!"

"Hey what?" asked Nicole.

"I just thought of a way to get Sam and the age machine back."

She'd been slumped on the couch, staring at my frayed rug. Now she had her head up, eyes shining. "How?"

"It's a bit on the complicated side. I'll explain when we get there."

"Get where?"

"Where we're going right now."

"But we're supposed to stay put until they contact us and tell us where to pick up Sammy."

I snorted. "Those lousy goons won't be contacting anybody. They'll sell the machine to Kane and knock off Sammy for laughs."

"But I hoped . . ."

"Hope is for suckers! And suckers don't win." I tossed the empty Scotch bottle in the wasteall and grabbed her hand. "C'mon, sister, let's hustle."

And we hustled.

To Chicago.

You guessed it. To Nate Oliver's lab.

He was fitting a tiny nearhair moustache to a plastolife cinema replica of Errol Flynn when we broke in on him.

"Hold it," he said tensely. "Three hairs to go."

We waited while he finished the job. Then, dusting his fat pink hands, he turned to face us. He stared at me, jowls wobbling.

"Hi, Nate."

"My goodness, Sam! What's happened to you? You've —you've aged."

"I'm seventy-one," I admitted. "Men get old."

His plump tongue scrubbed at his dry lips. He kept staring. "Do you—have some kind of—terrible disease?"

And he backed away a step.

I grinned. "Naw. I'm working the Umani caper from another universe. This is the third you I've dealt with on the case."

His cheeks puffed. "The *third* me?"

I nodded. "First I dealt with you in an earlier universe. In that one you tried to send me back home. In *my* world you time-snapped me out of some big trouble. Now I've come to see you again in *this* world. That's three yous all told."

Oliver digested this info, then blinked at Nicole. "And who is this young lady?"

"Her name is Nicole. They killed her in the universe you sent me to. The first you, I mean. See, you overshot me on that trip and I landed in . . ." He was looking a little green around the gills so I cooled my story. "Forget it, Nate. Just take my word I need help."

Oliver's face had fat beads of sweat all over it like raindrops on a window. "How—can I help you?"

"They've got the Sam you know, the one you thought I was. And they're going to kill him."

"And he's wet," Nicole cut in. "The poor thing needs a diaper change."

"How can a man in his thirties need a diaper change?" Nate wanted to know.

"He's just a brat now," I said. "We all got fouled up

135

with an age machine. It got out of hand, kind of, and reduced Sam to a six-month-old baby. Now they've got the machine and him with it."

"Who are they?"

"Three goons I killed back in my universe, except they're alive in *this* one."

Oliver slipped onto a stool, looking dazed.

"Here's the way it is," I said. "With me being over seventy the way I am I'm just not in shape to go hiking after those goonies."

"Granted," said Oliver. "But what has your physical condition to do with me?"

"You're my ace in the hole," I told him. "I'll bet you have some kind of universe transporter in your lab, right?"

"Wrong," he said with a wag of his wattles. "Closest thing is a rather balky time machine I'm fiddling with at present."

"That's bad news," I said. "If he could have moved me into just *one* more universe I could go get myself and bring me here and send myself after me. But now *that* idea is shot."

"Not really," said Nicole, looking wise. Beautiful and wise. She turned to Oliver. "You said you have a time machine. Just how efficient is it?"

He shrugged his puffy shoulders. "It won't project beyond a few weeks either way, past or future. I think there's a kink in it somewhere."

Nicole smiled brightly. "But that's long enough. We'll send Sam back in time—to last week—and we'll have him pick up your Sam *before* we turned him into a baby. Then we'll bring that adult Sam back here and send him after his future baby self!"

I scratched my cheek. "Sounds like a good plan," I agreed. "We can always send the other Sam back later—to his own week. Yeah, I think you've got it, Nicky!"

136

And I gave her a smack. She was a smart dame all right.

"You've never called me Nicky before," she said softly.

Oliver wasn't happy. "You shouldn't really go, really you shouldn't."

"Why not?"

"You could disarrange the structure of *our* present by going into our past. I get a jumpy feeling in the pit of my tummy just thinking about all that disarranged structure."

"Nuts!" I growled. "Forget your tummy and just get me into last week."

"You're a headstrong old man, Sam," Nate declared. "Headstrong old men have been the root-cause of mankind's darkest hours."

I said nuts again to that, and we walked into Nate's lab to have a go with his time machine.

It was spooky looking—a rickrack of bolts and hinged panels and glowing coils and plastic doohickies.

"Are you sure this thing will do the job?" I asked.

Nate spread his fat-palmed hands in the air helplessly. "One does one's best. I am sure it will transfer your physical body into last week. Beyond that, I'm not sure of anything."

"How about the return trip?" I said. "Can you get me and the other Sam back here okay?"

"My range is quite limited as to time pickups," he said. "But if you appear with him at the exact spot at which you are deposited and adhere to my schedule I don't think there'll be any problems."

"What's your schedule?"

"My machine works within certain set time phases. I will drop you at one time phase and pick you up at another. They can't be missed or we lose you."

"Meaning?"

"Meaning you must not only appear on the same spot

137

at which you exit but within a precise phase to be picked up. Didn't I just say that?" He was sweating again.

"I mean, how long will I have?"

Oliver said he'd need to check some data. He waddled away.

"I'm beginning to think my idea isn't worth the risk," Nicole said. She nibbled at a thumb.

"Don't bite your nails," I said. "Hate to see a woman biting her nails."

"Well, I'm nervous. Nate seems so—so uncertain of what he's sending you into."

"He's sending me into last week. I'll take care of the rest. We need another me to get myself back and that's that."

"All right,"Nicole sighed. "But I insist on going with you this trip. When you went after Esma you left me behind and I got into trouble."

I didn't like the setup. Still, the idea was hers and I needed to keep tabs on her. "Oke. You go with me."

She gave me a smile.

Oliver padded back waving a fistful of papers. "I have it all worked out mathematically," he said. "Time of departure, time of pickup, exit and re-entry—all phased out for you, Sam."

"For us," I corrected. "The girl goes with me."

Oliver nodded with a wobble of double chins. "Two are as easy to transport as one," he declared. "But the young lady's presence is required at this end."

Nicole looked startled. "Why?"

"To get us back. You see, my dear, I must go with Sam in order to make certain of the proper return-phase coordinates. They are vital to our success in re-entry. He could never manage it without me. We need you at this end."

"I see," she nodded. "Whatever's best."

"Good!" breathed Nate. "You'll have no difficulty in picking us up after I give you a few simple instructions."

He filled her in on the details while I prowled the lab, poking at test tubes and coiled wires. I was tensing up. Things were becoming too damn complex to suit me with all these alternate universes and dimensions to juggle. But I couldn't think of a better plan at the moment for getting Sammy back.

Nate said he was ready, and we sat down on two red bell-shaped seats within the body of the time machine.

Nicole leaned in to kiss me goodbye. "See you soon, lover."

"Yeah," I snapped, a little embarrassed. "Just don't get kidnapped or hypnotized while we're away."

She grinned, stepping back. Nate gave her some orders having to do with coordinates and junk.

"Better close your eyes, Sam," said Oliver. "Saves you from vertigo."

I did.

Nicole activated the time machine—and away we went into what I *hoped* was the middle of last week.

Twenty-Four

It was black. Deep black night. So dark I could see nothing. Yet I felt solid ground under me.

"Did we make it?" I asked.

"In a manner of speaking," Oliver replied.

"Better check our coordinates," I said.

"That's not necessary. We are in the proper time phase. I have no doubt that this is the middle of last week in terms of the week we left. But there *is* a problem I had not anticipated."

"What's that?" I asked.

"I'm all feathery," said Oliver. "And I have a beak and wings."

I gulped. My arms and hands were gone! I had just what Oliver had. "What the hell's happened?"

"The exit phase of our trip worked fine," said Oliver. "It was the entry phase that malfunctioned, as it were."

"What does that mean?"

"Simply that everything was hunkydory when we left *next* week. It was when we got here into *last* week that my machine kinked up."

"And turned us into birds?"

"Not birds, exactly. From what I can determine we are fishbirds, or Zubus. And we are on Pluto."

"But that's where I hunted Zubu eggs when the cop-mice brainwashed me."

"You will now, no doubt, be laying your own," said Oliver. His voice had a rather hollow tone, due to his having to talk through his beak.

"How can we do what we came here to do if we're a couple of Zubu birds?"

"The Zubu is not, strictly speaking, a bird—although it *looks* like one. It has fishy components."

I ruffled my neck feathers. "I don't give a damn about any of that crap! I'm a seventy-one-year-old-private detective from another universe stuck in the middle of last week inside the featherbrained body of a dumb bird who's really a fish and I—"

"Not *really* a fish," explained Oliver. "As I have attempted to point out to you—"

"All right," I said calmly. "Can we get back to Nicole?"

"At the proper pickup time," said Nate. "I don't think our being Zubus will affect the pickup. But that's at least two Earthdays away. We have plenty of time to hire your other self and transport him back with us, as planned."

"Who's going to listen to a big dumb featherheaded fishbird?"

"Oh, I'm sure you'll be able to explain things to Sam when we find him."

"And just how do we get from Pluto to Mars?"

"The way all other creatures of our universe do it, of course. We take a rocket."

I was upset with Nate's cool acceptance of our condition. He actually didn't seem to mind being a Zubu. But I let that pass. "Rockets cost," I told him. "And we don't have any credits to pay for a trip. And aren't we supposed to stay right here on Pluto and lay eggs and hide them?"

"You seem determined to approach our situation from a pessimistic viewpoint," scolded Oliver. He paddled back and forth in front of me on his flat webfeet, wings thoughtfully folded behind his back.

The black was thinning—or else I was becoming accustomed to it. At least I could see the landscape around us. No egg-hunting robots seemed to be in the area, which was a distinct relief. They'd be expecting us to bury some eggs for them to hunt and I didn't feel like getting into that whole depressing cycle if it could possibly be avoided.

Oliver was right. I *was* feeling very pessimistic about the whole case. I was a long way from Dr. Umani and Esma back in my own universe and there was no telling what had happened to them by now. F. could have murdered them both and destroyed the lab. Which could mean the end of the solar system.

"We'll never get aboard a Mars rocket," I said dejectedly, pecking at an interesting pebble on the ground. The pebble looked tasty so I swallowed it.

Being inside a fishbird was frustrating. Not that I was an unattractive Zubu; my feathers were neat and well oiled and my beak was long and graceful. It was losing my hands and arms that bugged me. Now I could see why Umani got so annoyed being inside a giraffehead.

Which reminded me of the old Venusian saying: unless you wear the rags of a Gork you cannot truly savor the soup of poverty.

"Why so negative?" Oliver asked. "We are intelligent individuals. We shall simply outsmart the rather slow-witted robot Zubu-keepers and stow our feathered bodies away on board a Mars rocket. With the proper team spirit we shall be successful. Have a little more faith in yourself, Sam."

"I'd have more faith in a loaded .38 right now," I said.

"Wit is a weapon far superior to a loaded gun," intoned Oliver through his beak.

I raised a wing. "Shhhh!" I said softly. "Here comes a night robot."

He clanked resolutely toward us, a big square iron fellow with blinking red bulb eyes and shiny brass arms.

142

"Hey, hey, hey," he said metallically, "you two Zubus shouldn't be out here in the middle of the dark talking. You should either be asleep with your beaks nestled in your downy feathers or you should be secretly burying your eggs. Which will it be?"

"Uh—we'll go to sleep," I told the blinking robot. "We've no eggs to bury."

"My feathered friend is correct," said Nate. "Sleep it will be."

The robot put his brass hands on his lips. "I'm waiting," he said.

I folded my thin stalk legs and flopped down. Then, taking my cue from what the robot had said, I bent my neck into a kind of S shape and buried my beak inside my under-wing feathers. It was suffocating and my beak tickled. I felt like sneezing.

Oliver was doing the same bit, folding down next to me.

"Sleep tight you two," said the robot, and he clanked heavily away, his red eyes fading in the darkness.

"Is he gone?" asked Oliver, who was afraid to lift his beak to find out.

"Yeah," I said, sneezing. "He's gone."

"Then let's sneak. Keep your beak down and sneak softly away."

We did that.

Reaching the edge of the Zubu grounds we encountered a robot gateguard.

"Now what?" I whispered.

"Get ready to waddle when I give the word," said Nate.

He scooped up a pebble in his beak and tossed it into the guardshack.

"Hah! The slow-witted fool is going inside to see what caused the noise," said Nate. "Now—*waddle!*"

When it has to, a Zubu can cover a lot of fast ground. I'd heard that it could waddle up to fifty miles an hour,

Earthspeed, which is fast waddling any way you cut it.

Paddling furiously, webfeet pumping, we were out the gate and down the road before the robot left his guard-shack.

"You know this terrain better than I do," panted Oliver as he waddled briskly beside me. "You've worked the area. How far to the rocketport?"

"About seven Earthmiles from this point," I said.

"We'll easily make it before daylight."

"How the hell do you know what time it is here on Pluto?" I asked him.

"By mentally checking one time phase against another." He paused in the road. "When does the next rocket leave for Bubble City?"

"One leaves every sixth Plutoperiod," I said.

"Then all we do is find out a good place to secrete ourselves until the next launch. Then we sneak craftily aboard with the baggage and sneak off again when we hit Bubble City."

"You make it sound dirt simple."

"It is. Just wait and see if it isn't."

It was. Easy. No one expected two feathery Zubus to smuggle themselves from Pluto to Mars so we had no problems. Besides, we were very crafty about the whole thing.

In Bubble City we did a fast waddle out to my office, Sam's office, and found me there behind the desk working a stack of case papers.

"Hello, Sam," I said.

"Hi there, Sam," Nate said.

Sam looked up and scowled. Here were two ragtag Zubus with ruffled feathers and bloodshot eyes standing in front of his desk. I knew he hated Zubu eggs (all the Sams did) and figured that Zubus were something less than stupid.

144

"Don't judge us by our appearance," warned Oliver. "We've had scant sleep and have been subjected to much bouncing and tossing amid the baggage of two planets."

"Right," I put in. "And, in fact, we are not Zubus at all."

Sam arched an eyebrow. "Then who are you?"

Nate spread his wings. "I am Nathan Oliver, your inventor friend from Chicago, and this—well, this is you, Sam, from another universe. At the moment we are forced to wear these bodies due to a scientific maladjustment in my time machine."

I came in behind Nate, talking fast to convince Sam we were legit. "Once we take you back to next week, where we started from, we'll be ourselves again." I dipped my beak into my chestfeathers and nibbled at an itch, then declared. "I'll be seventy-one next week."

"Happy birthday," Sam said coldly. "Now—will you two batty birds kindly get your tails out of my office. I'm busy."

Oliver gave me a sad look from his bloodshot left eye. "He doesn't believe us."

I paddled forward to face Sam. "Look, I know this is all a little tough to swallow but stick with me until I fill you in on the whole story. You won't regret it."

"What's in it for me?"

"A chance to earn some heavy gelt and a chance to save the System."

Sam pushed his stack of papers to one side and tented his hands on the desk. "Okay, bird, I'm listening."

"He really isn't a bird," Oliver said. "Not in a strict sense. The Zubu is actually a fascinating combination of—"

"Will you can that crap!" I snapped. "I've got to convince Sam we're on the level and you're *not* helping."

"Sorry," mumbled Oliver, scuffing a webfoot against the office floor. "You go ahead. I'll keep my beak shut."

"Good!" I turned back to Sam and was about to begin

my explanation when I was seized with an overwhelming urge. I tried to resist but the urge got stronger by the second. "First, before I continue, I'm afraid I am going to have to lay an egg," I told Sam. "That's just the way it is."

"Okay, but lay it fast."

"Egg-laying is not a matter of speed," I informed him. "A Zubu lays when the urge is upon him. As soon as my urge builds to its completion my egg will be laid."

"How long?"

I raised my beak. "Can't say."

We all waited. Sam rocked back in his chair, tapping the desktop nervously with an index finger. Nate watched me, frankly curious, since he'd probably be laying an egg of his own before we left the office.

I waddled over to Sam's couch, sat down on it, carefully arranging my feathers.

"Snap it up," Sam ordered.

"Stand by," I said. "Get ready. Now!" The freckled egg magically appeared beneath me on the couch. I was proud of it. I'd never laid one before and it was a real accomplishment. Not every private eye gets to lay his own egg.

"It's good looking, isn't it?" I asked Nate.

He lowered his downy head to inspect it. "Sure is, Sam. That's a real beaut."

"Forget the damn egg and tell me what you came to tell me," growled Sam.

"First I've got to hide it," I said. "After a Zubu lays he feels a real need to hide his egg. I've got to fulfill that need."

Sam had lost patience. "You two birds better just breeze out. I don't have any more time to waste on Zubu eggs. I *hate* Zubu eggs to begin with."

"We hate what we don't understand," said Nate. "That is man's eternal curse."

"Breeze!"

146

Oliver spread his wings in supplication. "We cannot leave, Mr. Space. Please give my friend a chance to convince you."

"Close your eyes," I said to Sam.

"You must be kidding."

"No. I can't let you watch me hide it. If you close your eyes I can hide it quickly and then get on with my story."

Sam, snorting angrily, closed his eyes.

I hid the egg under the couch. "Okay, you can open up," I said.

"Now talk," Sam said.

I talked.

Twenty-Five

Sam emptied the Scotch bottle, wiped his lips, and put the bottle on the desk. "All rightie," he said. "Let's see if I've got it all straight. You want to hire me to come with you into next week so that I can run down myself as a kidnapped six-month-old brat. Is that it?"

"That's it," I said, rapidly nodding my beak. "Once you've brought back your future self—along with the age machine and our transporter hats—we'll have the basic situation under control."

"Then we'll return you here, to your proper time zone," added Oliver.

"And how do you pay me? In Zubu eggs?"

I shook my downy head. "Not at all. We'll pay you in normal solarcredits once we get back into our bodies."

"And what if I get stuck in next week?"

"You won't," Oliver assured him. "We have faith in your ability to re-capture yourself."

"It is absolutely the nuttiest case I've ever taken," Sam said. "It's me hiring me to find me. When I show up with you characters we'll have three of me in next week!"

Oliver web-paddled close to the desk. "Are we to understand you are taking the case?"

"Yeah, you are to understand that," Sam growled. "Hell, I've got a personal stake in the thing. If I don't find myself I'm in trouble. It's like sending my left foot after my right foot."

148

"A perfectly logical way to regard the case," agreed Oliver.

"When can we make our pickup?" I asked Nate. "The longer we stay here the worse things get."

"Not in the sense you mean," said Oliver. "Since the future hasn't happened yet it can't get any worse while we remain here in the past."

"I still want to know when we can leave. I hate wearing feathers and laying eggs."

Oliver did some rapid calculation in his head. "We are now in the tenth time phase and we need to be in the eleventh, at the very earliest, for a pickup."

"When does the next phase start?"

"If we take a rocket to Neptune we should just about hit it square on."

I shook my beak. "No more baggage holds for me. That's out."

"There's a Zubu base on Neptune. Sam can take us there as escaped Zubus, claiming that he was hired by the company to turn us in as fugitive fishbirds. We'll go aboard the rocket with our wings shackled, as his prisoners. Once on Neptune we phase in and bingo! we pop back into the middle of next week."

"Sounds ok to me," said Sam.

"I'll buy it," I said. Actually, I didn't fancy having my wings shackled but it sure beat playing stowaway.

Oliver ruffled his tail feathers. "Then we'll leave momentarily."

"Why not now?" Sam asked.

"First, I have to lay a speckled egg. Second, I have to hide my egg. *Then* we can leave." He gave us both a long look along his beak. "And no peeking!"

What with the cold temp, the poisonous gases and the hostile treatment we were getting as runaways, it was pleasant to pop off of Neptune on Nicole's time-phase

149

pickup beam. She worked it like a pro, and we got back into next week without a hitch. And as ourselves. I was still seventy-one but we'd fix that later.

Sam took off after the three goons, telling Nicole and me to wait for him in Bubble City.

Which we did.

In an Earthday Sam was back, carrying his baby self, the age machine and our two portahats.

"He needs a change," said Sam.

Nicole clucked like a mother hen. "I'll take him."

Sammy was bawling like crazy and I asked Nicole where she was going to find a diaper.

"I can jury-rig one from part of my clothing," she said. "And if the age machine is still working properly we shouldn't need more than one."

As she was changing Sammy I asked Sam if he'd had any problems.

"Sure," he nodded. "You always get problems in a kid caper. If you try to close in on the goons they might finish off the kid before you can reach him. You have to handle it cautious."

"Well, where did you run 'em down?"

"I traced 'em to one of the dogstar asteroids where they were hiding Sammy and took 'em by surprise. They turned over Sammy and the other junk on my word I'd let 'em go."

"And you let 'em go?"

Sam snorted. "Hell, no. I shot all three of them after I had the kid. You don't play square with gungoons."

"Check," I said, "and double check."

"There's the little sweetums," cooed Nicole, and put freshly-changed Sammy on the couch. We got the age machine humming.

Little Sam began to age. His bones lengthened; his hair sprouted; his face filled out . . . By the time we turned off the machine we had a thirty-six-year-old private eye in a homemade diaper facing us.

He was too stunned to say anything.

"Bring him some clothes," I told Nicole. "Then get me back to normal."

This time we did it right, and I was thirty-six again. It felt great.

So there we were: three Sam Spaces, all the same guy, all thirty-six. Three ugly, mean-looking mugs.

"What now?" the first Sam asks.

The second Sam, the one we'd popped out of last week, looked confused. "Now we split, right?"

I nodded. "You go back to Chicago where Nate will take care of you. He'll see you safely into last week."

"As a Zubu?"

"Naw. He's got the kink out of his equipment. You'll be back there as yourself." I fished a stack of credits from my coat. "With these."

"Thanks, Sam," he said, grinning. "I feel a little queasy, taking money from myself."

"Nerts," I said. "You sure as hell earned it."

Nicole gave him a peck on the cheek and he left.

"What about me?" asked the other Sam.

"You just stay here where you belong," I told him, putting on a portahat and helping Nicole with hers. "We're going to high-tail it back home and find out what's happened to Doc Umani. Hey—what about *your* Umani? You're on the case, aren't you?"

"Not any more," he said. "Umani took me off a few days back. Said he could handle his own protection."

The vidphone buzzed. Sam snapped it on. "Space here," he said.

The image on the vidscreen belonged to a sobbing Esma. She was shaking and her words were choked. "They—they got him, Sam!"

"Who?"

"Kane's men. Synthetics. They've kidnapped Daddy!"

"Hang tight, sister, and I'll be right over."

151

I sighed. "Somebody is always getting kidnapped in this caper."

"Yeah," he said, snapping on his .38 and heading for the door. "At least it pays the rent."

By the time he hit the street we were back in our own universe.

In time to meet fresh trouble.

Twenty-Six

"Where have you been?" asked Esma as we entered Umani's lab. "I've been calling your office about Daddy."

"Don't tell me. He's been kidnapped. Right?"

"It's much worse than that," she said.

"He's dead," I nodded. "Some goons nailed him."

"Oh, no. Worse than dead." Her three sets of eyes looked desperate.

"What's worse than dead?" I wanted to know.

"Daddy has gone cuckoo," she told me. "Totally bonkers as of yesterday."

"Tell me all about it," I said, walking to a chair, flipping it around and straddling it. I was alone with Esma. Nicole was resting in New Old New Mexico where she'd gone after we got back. She needed a vacation from crime and criminals and she picked out an automated dude ranch near Sante Fe to do her resting in. I told her I'd join her just as soon as I saved the System.

It was no joke. I had to make certain Umani succeeded with his experiment—even if it meant round-the-clock guard duty. I'd come to this conclusion based on Kane's attempt to put me out of action.

So here I was, being told the doc had gone bonkers.

"Everything seemed fine yesterday morning," said Esma. "We were working in the lab, Daddy and I, when—"

"Where was first cousin Verlag?"

"Oh, Daddy killed him."

153

I gave with the arched eyebrow. "Why?"

"You remember how grouchy he was?"

"Yeah, he did a lot of dark scowling."

"Well," said Esma, "he began getting on Daddy's nerves. Kept muttering and scowling and grouching around."

"That's no reason to freeze him."

"No, of course not. But he got worse. Began neglecting his lab duties and padded around the building carrying an unsheathed Japanese battle sword."

"Authentic?"

"A replica. But very sharp and deadly."

"Go on."

"Day before yesterday he tried to chop off Daddy's head."

"And your father killed him?"

"Not then. He chopped off Daddy's head with no trouble at all. Japanese battle swords are very effective. When I arrived on the scene Verlag was standing over Daddy and chuckling. It was good to see him happy and smiling but certainly not at the cost of Daddy's head."

"I can see your point."

"I gave him a good tongue lashing and told him to go fetch a fresh coldpac from storage."

"Did he?"

"Sure. He was a bit sheepish about what he'd done.

I brain-switched Daddy into the body of an ex-Armenian rug peddler and things seemed to be straightened out."

"How can he be an ex-Armenian?"

"My error." She smiled. "I put my ex in the wrong place. I should have said an Armenian ex-rug peddler. Anyhow, that's who I put Daddy into."

"Ok. Then what?"

"Daddy was understandably miffed at Verlag and took away the Japanese battle sword. Then Verlag attacked

154

Daddy with an elephant's foot umbrella stand. Replica, of course."

"Figures," I nodded. "You can't get a genuine elephant's foot umbrella stand these days."

"At any rate," continued Esma, "Verlag's attack was foiled and Daddy shot him to death."

"Any reason for the attack?"

"I think Kane sent one of his hypnothetics to work on Verlag. He just wasn't rational."

"And then, after cooling Verlag, your Daddy went bonkers?"

"Not immediately. For awhile we worked on his experiment together. Then, when we were nearing total success, Daddy began jumping around the lab demanding rugs to sell. I told him we didn't have any rugs on Mars. But he was stubborn about the demand."

"I'd say the Armenian body was affecting his sanity."

Esma nodded two of her heads, still talking with the third. "That's what *I* thought. Though no other body had affected him to such a degree. Anyway, to be on the safe side, I brain-switched him to the body of an English instructor from West Redding, Connecticut. That seemed to work fine—but then Daddy got extremely interested in the alcoholic behavioral patterns of the major American writers of the 20th Century and abandoned his lab duties."

"So you switched him again?"

"He wouldn't let me. He defrosted all the coldpacs and that left us without spares. Next he took Verlag's Japanese battle sword and began hacking away at his experiment. That was yesterday. I managed to deal with him in time to save the lab. Knocked him unconscious with the elephant's foot umbrella stand and locked him in the storageunit. He's there now."

"I'd better talk to him," I said.

"I hope you can discover what's happened to Daddy. I

155

can't finish the experiment without him. His brain holds the key."

"I'll do my best."

She led me to the rear of the labunit and nodded her middle head toward a stout nearoak door, bolted from the outside. "He's in there. Be careful."

I patted my coat. "Got my .38 in case he gets violent," I told her.

The doc's voice filtered through the door. "Is that you, Esma? Who's with you?"

"It's Mr. Space, Daddy. He's come to talk to you."

"Splendid," we heard Umani say. "I am, in point of fact, a starving man."

"But I fed you just an hour ago. Beans, potatoes and nearhash."

"Quite so," agreed the doc. "But *that* was physical food which feeds only the body. I require mental food which feeds the soul. And my soul is starving."

Esma sighed as she unbolted the door. "See," she said sadly. "Bonkers."

"You stay here, " I told her. "I want to talk to him alone. I won't be long."

Umani was seated on a scrolled antique trunk, wearing a plastosilk dressing gown with puffy fur slippers on his feet. His new body was dapper and distinguished looking with a gray pencil moustache and trim goatee. He shook my hand firmly and offered me the free half of the trunk. I sat down.

"Try to remember," I said. "Did anyone come in and hypnotize you recently?"

"My, what a shallow opening question," he clucked. "If I were hypnotized I should certainly not be aware of it. Your question is akin to asking an insane man if he remembers going crazy."

"Right," I agreed. "But we don't have much time, and I was trying to shock you back to normal with a direct question."

"What is normal?" he asked tartly.

"Normal," I said, "is when you go back to work on your experiment and save our solar system."

Umani tipped his head back and laughed. His goatee wobbled with glee. "Well, well, well," he chuckled. "So I'm a universe-saver am I?"

"Nope. Only a solar-system saver. The universe itself is ok as far as I know."

"And just who am I outwitting with my system-saving?"

"I'm not going to go into all that," I said. "You either know or you don't. Obviously, right now, you're abnormal. There's no use trying to educate you."

"Splendid," and Umani snapped his fingers. "Instead, let me educate you. I'm a teacher, you know."

"So Esma told me. The pride of West Redding."

"Indeed. Esma is a delightful child. But I do wish she would not lock people up in storage units. It is quite annoying."

"Look, I'd better—"

"My current in-depth research project centers in and around the subject of excessive alcoholic intake among leading 20th Century authors."

"I'm no reader," I said. "I don't follow that kind of stuff."

"Ah, but the facts are absolutely fascinating. Did you know, for example, that after William Faulkner received news of his having won the Nobel Prize for Literature he got dead drunk in the woods of Mississippi? Took him several days to sober up enough to travel to Sweden for the award."

"So he liked to belt a few."

"Indeed he did. Hemingway ruined his liver by drinking. He used to drink with bears. Finally shot himself, of course. Sad. Then there was Dylan Thomas. Eighteen straight whiskies finished him off in New York. Steinbeck was notorious for his prolonged alcoholic bouts."

157

I tried to get up but he put a strong hand on my shoulder.

"Norman Mailer stabbed one of his wives while under the influence," he said. "And poor Scott Fitzgerald was a terrible lush."

"I don't want to hear any more guff about soused writers," I said, grabbing Umani by the front of his robe. I shook him furiously. "Wake up, doc! Come to your senses! You've got the whole damn System to save!"

I was still trying to shake some sense into him when Esma—shouting like an Oriental demon—launched herself through the door and attacked me with the Japanese battle sword.

Twenty-Seven

It was a tricky situation. When the battle blade sliced Umani's scrolled antique trunk neatly in half I knew I'd have to do something fast. Esma was dead set on cutting off my head and I had to deal with her.

She was in the midst of an overhand swing when I socked three .38s into her midriff.

She dropped the heavy sword, rattled, gurgled, sputtered. Her eyes pinwheeled in her heads, and she spun in a circle, saying, "Sam. Sam. Sam. Sam. Sam. Sam."

Then she flopped over one of the other trunks.

"Well done, sir!" said Umani, emerging from a corner. He dusted himself and combed out his goatee. "My daughter was quite insane. I should have realized that when she locked me in here. Wouldn't listen to anything I had to say. She was quite unsettled."

"Hmmmm," I murmured, bending over her body.

"She claimed I was hypnotized," said Umani. "Preposterous!"

"You *are* hypnotized," I said. "And it was Esma who did it."

"Why would my own daughter hypnotize me?"

"She's not your daughter." I unscrewed a finger, held it up. "She's a robot—a dupe of the real Esma, no doubt sent here by Kane to lure me into this place and behead me while I talked with you."

159

"Then where is Esma, the *real* Esma?"

"Dunno," I said. "I'll try and find her. People are always disappearing on me."

Umani shook his head, one hand pressed to his cheek. "It's—wearing off. My sense is returning."

"The effects ended with the destruction of the robot," I said. "This Esma android must have tranced Verlag into attacking you to get rid of him. Then she tranced you."

Umani swung toward the lab. "My experiment! Have they destroyed it?"

I followed him into the labunit. He darted here and there, checking this, checking that. Then he sighed and nodded. "Everything seems to be in order—at the near-final stage in which I left it."

"Good," I said. "When can you finish?"

"Within twenty-four hours."

"Ok. I'll stick with you the whole time. No use taking any more risks."

"But what about Esma?"

"Our System comes first. I'll go after her as soon as I know the planets and moons are all acey-deucey."

Umani beckoned me over to a high deepshelf. "You won't be required to search for Esma. I've found her."

And he had. She'd been bound, with gags on her three mouths. We got her down and stripped off the gags.

"It was Kane," she gasped with her nearest head. "Two of his synthos did this to me. They said they'd be back to collect me later."

"If they try, all they'll collect is a .38 smack in the belly," I said.

"Excellent!" enthused Umani. "A superb expression of brute-male ego-strength. I'm *sure* Norman Mailer would have liked you."

"Let's discuss my brute-male ego-strength some other time," I snapped. "You hop to your test tubes, doc.

160

There's no telling when Kane intends to set off his solar-busting operation."

"Oh, but there is," said Esma, untangling herself from the last of the nearcord ropes.

"There is what?"

"A way to tell when Kane intends to destroy the System."

"Spill it."

"I overheard one of his robots tell another that it would be strange living outside the System. And the second one said yes, it would, but he'd better get used to the idea because by stage 27 they'd be on their way."

I did some rapid calculation and sucked in a worried breath.

Umani squinted at me. "What's wrong, Mr. Space?"

"Stage 27 is how they number the days on Venus," I said. "Today is stage 26. Which means that by tomorrow, Venus time, the System is scheduled to blow."

"Then we're lost," declared Umani. "There's no time for me to complete my experiment."

"Maybe I can get to Venus and stop Kane," I said. "I could book a warper out tonight and be there by stage 26 and a half with luck."

"How would you find Kane? And how would you be able to stop him?" asked Umani.

"I'll find him all right. Kane's an easy man to trace. As for stopping him, I couldn't do it alone. Best I can do is divert him and buy you enough time." I put my hand on his shoulder. "Keep working. Round the clock. No sleep. No time out for food. Esma can feed you while you work."

"I'll do as you say," nodded the doc.

"We just might beat out Kane's timetable," I said. "I'll try and stall him somehow. If you can neutralize his operation before he can set off his chain-reaction the System won't blow. It's a chance."

"But, Sam," Esma protested. "You'll never come out alive. Not this time."

"It's my gamble, sister," I told her. "Stay with Daddy. I've got a warper to catch."

The pot was coming to a boil. When I landed on Venus I didn't waste a second. Three vizcalls and I'd located Kane's Venusian hangout—a plush playpalace deep in the jungles of Sazz at the western edge of Lake Desire.

Sazz was off-limits to tourists, an ancient hunting ground sacred to the Venusian people. Lake Desire was reserved for gleeking. Gleeks provided food and clothing for the natives of Sazz the way the buffalo did for the Plains Indian way back when. Gleeks were immense furry wingfish living in Lake Desire's natural-gas environment. They looked terrible yet tasted fine.

I got my official permission to go inland at government headquarters.

"You don't smell nearly as bad as most of your people," commented the clerk as he affixed an official seal and stamped my clearcard. He lowered a green tentapod in my direction, sniffing gently. Venusians have extremely sensitive smellers and I'd showered on the warper in order not to offend. They claim that Earthbodies give off an unpleasant scent and I was doing my best to avoid insulting the natives.

The clerk told me that it was a strange time of year to be visiting Lake Desire. I agreed, telling him that I'd traced a fugitive Capellan onion-smuggler into the jungles near the lake and had to capture him. It was my job, I said.

"Then may you have success and father many piggims," smiled the clerk.

That was the Venusian form of goodbye and I told him I hoped he'd father many piggims also. He wrinkled a fusia-tinted centipod at me in the traditional gesture of good luck and I stuck my tongue out at him as a sign of respect for his office.

Then I was free to go.

A jungle slicer took me into Sazz country and I switched to a personal jumpcart for the run into Lake Desire. They called it that because of the weirdly erotic effect it had on all males. When you flew over you got an erection. As simple as that. No matter what planet you were from as long as you had a penis it got erect over Lake Desire. One of nature's many quirks.

Just beyond the western tip of the lake I spotted Kane's playpalace buried in the thick jungle below me.

I cut along the edge of the lake, watching the giant gleeks glide through the gas like bats in a cave, trying to figure a way to land close enough to Kane's layout without being spotted.

The power-unit coughed and quit cold on my junper.

The figuring was over. I was heading down. Now.

Funny thing: here I was gliding into a death trap and the only thing I could think of was how I could lose my desire.

It was damned embarrassing, dropping out of the sky on my arch-enemy, Ronfoster Kane, with a full erection.

Twenty-Eight

Luckily, Kane's layout was far enough inland from the erotic waters of Lake Desire to allow my lust to subside by the time I crash-landed in his patio.

Ronfoster Kane was there to greet me, all seven feet of him, his jeweled teeth exposed in a smile of pure delight. He wore a floor-length tile and teak sliprobe and his steel hands were encased in unborn duckfur mittens. He bowed to me. "How fortunate that you should drop in, Mr. Space. I was loath to leave the System without personally attending to your torture and death."

"It's always nice to be welcome," I said.

The jumper was beat up plenty. A giant potted Venusian Mongoose bush had absorbed most of the impact. A Mongoose is the toughest domestic plant in the System. My right elbow was sore from the crash and I'd scraped a couple of knuckles. Otherwise I'd survived intact.

I wondered how long I'd stay that way.

More important yet: how much time could I buy for Umani?

"We might as well start your torture immediately," said Kane, consulting his wristcron. "I'm on a tight schedule."

He waved, and two burly synthos grabbed my arms. "Ouch!" I said. "Easy on the elbow."

"But these are my two chief torturers," declared Kane. "It won't do you a whit of good to tell them not to hurt you. They are *designed* to hurt people."

"I've got some info you'd like to have," I said to Kane. "Let's talk."

"Our talk is done," said Kane. He turned to the robots. "Take him to the Chamber of Pain and give him the works."

"Wait a sec," I said—and palm-chopped one of the snythos while I knee-popped the other. They let me go. "Listen to me," I said as the two frustrated robots rushed back to have another go, "I bet you'd like to know how I managed to disappear so neatly last time when you thought you had me cooked."

I side-stepped the robots' charge and danced around the Mongoose plant. "Well—wouldn't you?"

Kane nodded, his all-black eyes flashing with curiosity. "As a matter of fact, I *would* like to know now that you bring up the matter."

"Okay," I said, hopping between rows of standing sweetnose plants. "But first, call off your synthos."

Kane waved them back. They took up wary positions near the patio door. "All right, Space. Be quick. Proper torturing takes time and I *do* want them to get at it. You just wouldn't believe my schedule."

I sat down on a spreading nutweed and rubbed my sore elbow. "Boy, this hurts."

"You have exactly one millisecond to begin or I turn you back over to my synthetics," snapped Kane. "How *did* you disappear?"

"Keep your mittens on," I said, "and I'll tell you. It has to do with my red-haired girl friend, Nicole, and a solar agent's transporter hats. She turned up with the trick hats and we used 'em to pop ourselves into another universe."

"How dull," sighed Kane. "I thought I might learn something of vital interest if I delayed your torture."

In a panic now, I tried another stall. "Don't you want to know how I found you? Or how I got here?"

"No, they can torture that kind of info out of you. I've no more time to waste. To talk is to dawdle."

Kane waved me into the grip of the two synthos. "Take him. Quickly!"

I sputtered, tried some more words on Kane. He wasn't listening.

They dragged me away.

The Chamber of Pain was down a long winding flight of damp stairs, suitably cobwebbed. All proper torture chambers are at the bottom of damp cobwebbed stairs and Kane had spared no expense with this one. It had iron maidens, toe-crusher boots, spiked gloves, glowing-hot head bands and a bone-stretching bodyrack which one of the torture boys told me was the latest model.

"It's self-adjusting," he said. "Powered entirely by atomic vibration, with a full year's parts-and-labor guarantee."

"Sounds like a fair deal," I said.

"It will handle any creature in the System, human or non-human," said the second syntho. "We just set the dial and it does the job. Takes all the work out of bone-stretching."

"Your boss really does things in a big way," I said.

"He's no penny-pincher," said the first torturer, fitting an iron skull-thumper on my head.

"What's this?"

"We thought we'd start with a few sharp thumps to the skull," said the second torturer. "We just got this in and haven't had a chance to try it out yet. Do you mind?"

"Suit yourself," I shrugged. "Torture is torture."

"Oh, but that's not true at all," said the first syntho. "Torture can vary considerably. There's torture by water, by fire, by rawhide strips, by whip, by fist and by club—just to name a few basic types. Naturally, we prefer to use more inventive methods."

"Naturally," I said.

"This is going to be a good satisfactory session," said the second torturer, slapping his hands together. "I think we'll all get a lot out of it."

"I'm sure it'll be a kick in the head for me," I said. But they didn't get the joke. Synthos are singularly lacking in humor. Well, I didn't like getting thumped sharply on the skull. It gave me a hell of a headache.

I wondered what they'd use on me next.

"After a few more thumps we'll probably switch to a bone-crushing unit. Ever had your bones crushed into a fine white powder?"

"Not that I can recall," I said.

"You won't like it," said the torturer. "But it's colorful."

"For a couple of machines you bozos seem to take a lot of sadistic pleasure in your jobs."

"Oh, yes, indeed we do!" said the second syntho. "But that's how Kane designed us. We're just functioning according to design. If we giggle when we put you on the rack that's just normal with us."

They'd injected me with a no-will shot. Meaning I had absolutely no will to resist. I could feel pain—but the will to resist it was removed. I was docile and totally non-violent. The thought of having my bones ground into powder amused me. No terror or fear was involved.

"I don't like this new skull-thumper," said the first syntho as he removed it from my head. "Has no lasting pain potential."

"Agreed," said the second. "Let's get Space into the crusher unit. That's really a keen item."

They were strapping me into the unit when the door bounced open and Nicole popped in, a Webber-Standish .88 tribeam hacker in her right fist. She fired two bolts into my synthetic friends. Then she unstrapped me.

"Say," I remarked, "I thought you were relaxing in New Old New Mexico."

"I was. But I got jaded. I needed action. Esma told me where you'd gone."

"How'd you get in?"

"Back way. I landed in the jungle—after an alarmingly erotic trip over the lake—and shot my way inside."

I nodded. "Ok. And thanks. Kane was getting ready to blow up the solar system. We'd better find out what's happening."

We stepped over the dead synthos and crept upstairs, looking for the Robot King. He was in the library, alone and unguarded.

I didn't get it.

"Kane, you should be surrounded by synthos. What's the idea?"

He laughed, his ruby and diamond molars flashing rainbow patterns on the library ceiling.

"He's not at all upset at our being here," said Nicole. "Sam, I don't like this."

"Would you like to ask me some questions?" said Kane.

"Yeah, one just came to mind," I said. "How come you're still on Venus? You've got to clear out of the System before you can blow it apart. Yet you're still here."

Kane folded his mittened hands. "I must be here and so must Nicole. We are the catalysts which will move the plan into its final phase."

Nicole looked stunned. "You mean, I'm *supposed* to be here? You knew I was coming to rescue Sam?"

"Of course," smiled Kane. "F. had to have us both here at this precise time and place in order to fuse our metallic substances in a charge which sets off the chain reaction which starts each of the nine planets moving into final collision orbit."

I blinked dumbly at Kane. "But—*you're* F.—aren't you?"

"No, Mr. Space. But F. took great pains to make you believe I was." He opened his sliprobe and unzipped a

168

section of his chestskin. Wires and tubes. "As you can now see, the Robot King is himself a robot."

I swung toward the girl. "And—Nicole . . ."

Kane nodded. "She too. There has never been a flesh-and-blood Nicole."

"I don't believe you," she screamed. "I'm human. I *know* I am!"

Kane grabbed the front of her servoblouse and ripped it away from her body. He dug steel hands into her flesh.

I watched, lacking the will to interfere.

Her chest revealed the truth. Wires and tubes.

Nicole fell back, sobbing. The tribeam hacker slipped from her fingers to the floor. I looked at it numbly.

Kane levered his tall body toward me. "Do you begin to see now, Mr. Space? F. brought us together here for the sole purpose of uniting certain metallic elements in our cunningly-fashioned robobodies. Once united, these elements will interact and set off the final phase."

"Not if I destroy both of you here and now," I said.

"Ah, but you lack the will to destroy anything or anybody. I saw to that when I had my synthos drug you. F. greatly admires you, Mr. Space. He wanted you in on the final moments to witness his master triumph."

"How do you unite with the girl?" I asked, still looking at the tribeam weapon. Nicole had fallen into a chair, still sobbing.

"Simple. We merely press our left hands together and the substances are joined. Thus!"

He reached for Nicole's limp hand. She offered no resistance.

"Say goodbye to your solar system, Mr. Space. F. has won!"

And, at the moment, it looked as if he had.

169

Twenty-Nine

Nate was surprised to see me. He asked me what I was doing in Chicago.

"Saving our solar system," I told him.

"That's *some* reason to be in Chicago!"

I explained the whole situation to him, filling him in on what had happened back on Venus.

"Then you managed to destroy the Kane and Nicole robots before they could touch hands?"

"Obviously," I said, "or we wouldn't be here right now. The no-will drug wore off at the last possible second and I was able to put them both out of action. But I haven't stopped F. He'll be triggering the operation from beyond the System. No telling where that would be. Without you, there's no way to stop him."

"I'm reconstructing Charles Laughton's stomach right now," said Nate. "Then I have John Wayne's buttocks to refurbish."

"Forget all that stuff," I snapped. "The whole System depends on you now."

"Keep talking," said Nate as we walked into his lab.

"At the present moment F. is totally beyond my reach. He's holed up somewhere in deep space. But, with you behind me, I know how to nail him."

"Another time jump I bet!"

I nodded. "Yeah. I need to have you pop me back to where I was *before* I left for Venus this last time. That

170

way I can still grab F. *before* he leaves for deep space. You get me?"

"Oh, I get you all right," Nate said. "Fact is, I'm pretty handy with time jumps now. Got all the bugs out."

"Great," I said, climbing into his time rig. "You'll be remembered as the man who saved our solar system, Nate!"

The last thing I saw was Nate's pink blush of pleasure as I was zapped into the recent past.

Mars.
Umani's lab just before I cut for Venus.
Perfect.

"Well, don't just stand there, Sam," said Esma. "Aren't you going to Venus to stop Kane?"

"I've *been* there—and I've stopped Kane. Now I'm stopping the evil genius behind Ronfoster Kane."

Esma raised three sets of eyebrows. "I don't understand."

"You wouldn't, baby. You never have. If you had understood what was really happening around you, Esma, you'd never have allowed yourself to become an unwitting pawn in the slimy hands of F."

"What are you saying to me?"

Doc Umani pressed the cold round barrel of a Spanner-Wassleman .420 FJ whipcharge prober into the small of my back. "Sam is telling you that you've been played for a silly little three-headed fool, my dear." He chuckled. "Correct, Mr. Space?"

"Correct," I said tightly.

"But I don't see—" Esma blinked rapidly, unable to put it all together.

"Even you, his adopted daughter, were totally unaware that the brain you kept switching safely from body to body was that of Sir Henry Fasterfaster, otherwise known as F. Looks as if you had us all fooled, Sir Henry."

Esma slumped down onto a research stool. "But—if Daddy is F. why was he working on an experiment to counter-act his own plan to destroy the System?"

"Can you answer her, Space?"

"Of course. He only *told* us that the work he was doing involved *saving* the System. It was what they call in my biz a cover story—allowing him to work openly on his real plan of total destruction."

"Why was he always under attack? Who was attacking him?"

"Sir Henry built Kane and empowered the robot to simulate attacks against him. Note I said simulate—for your pseudo-Daddy was never entirely dead. You were always able to effect a safe brain-switch. He kept you around for that purpose. The rest was all fakery to avoid possible suspicion from other legit scientists who might have cracked wise to him."

"But—why did he hire you?"

"For the same reason. By sending his own hired detective on a wild goose chase around the System he maintained his innocent image, leaving him free to continue his work. Also, don't overlook the fact that Sir Henry is a fiendish sadist. He got a sick kind of kick out of seeing me chase my tail."

"Indeed I did," chuckled Sir Henry. "And Nicole's detailed reports of your colorful lovemaking delighted me immensely. Nicole was a *perfect* robot, was she not, Mr. Space?"

This time it was my turn to blush. And I don't blush easy.

"Why did he kill Verlag?"

"Because ole Verlag got onto his *real* work—and was threatening to expose him to me. F. faked insanity and killed Verlag to shut him up."

Esma glared at him with her six green eyes. "I'm glad I'm no blood kin of yours!" she spat. "At least my real three-headed Venusian daddy was honest and good."

172

"Pah!" snorted Sir Henry. "Goodness makes me puke! Being evil is all kinds of fun. Like blowing up solar systems. Sheer fun all the way!" He prodded me with the prober. "To properly satisfy my evil impulses, Mr. Space, I shall ask you to personally strangle my goody-goody adopted daughter. I have no further use for her and I'm sick of her prattle. You may begin with the neck on the left."

I tensed my fighting muscles. "And why should I do what you tell me to do?"

"If you don't, I blast you where you stand."

I turned to face him. My voice was ice; my fists were balled and ready. "That's easy to say, you evil bastard! But you build robots to do your killing for you. Man to man, when the chips are down, I say you haven't got the guts to pull a trigger!"

I was wrong about that. He *had* the guts.

He pulled the trigger.

And I was dead.

But, in almost the same Earthinstant, so was F.

A .38 nitrocharge Colt-Wesson thundered from the door, exploding Sir Henry's evil brain. The distinguished body from West Redding, Connecticut, proved to be his last abode.

"Sam!" cried Esma, throwing herself into my eager arms.

Yeah, it was me. I'd arrived in time to do a chill job on F.—thanks to ole Nate.

I mean, the me that's telling you this story arrived. The *other* me, the very dead one, was also zapped here by Nate but he played it dumb and got himself knocked off. It was up to me to save Esma.

Obviously *I'm* not dead, or I wouldn't be telling this story.

But, in another sense, they're *all* me. All the Sam Spaces out there gunning their way through all those alternate universes. Some of them buy the big sleep, some don't. You play the odds.

Esma was still plenty confused.

"I don't think you've tied up all the loose ends," she said.

"I'm sure I haven't," I said, holstering the .38 and squeezing her waist.

She was warm and willing in my arms.

Making it with a three-headed babe is no cinch. But like I said way back in the beginning, a lush Venusian triplehead turns me on.

"Sam, you are remarkable," she admitted. "I just hope no more of you show up."

"Right now, sister, one of me's enough," I said.

And proved it.

174